THE LAST WAR

ANNE ELIZABETH WINCHELL

Part of this work was previously published in 2010 by Texas State University as a Masters of Fine Arts dissertation entitled *The Last War*.

ISBN-13: 978-1-9449-6904-2

Cover design by Anne Winchell

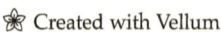 Created with Vellum

To my wonderful parents and everything they've done to help me pursue my dreams

ACKNOWLEDGMENTS

Thank you to my parents, who have encouraged me in everything that I do. I would also like to thank Debra Monroe, my thesis advisor, who helped develop this novel. Teya Rosenberg and John Blair also offered valuable insights and helped me catch numerous mistakes throughout the writing process. Finally, thank you to Lily and Laura, my two friends in this publishing adventure.

PROLOGUE

Medane ran through the deserted streets of London, his steps echoing against broken windows and collapsed buildings. He was out of breath. His genetically enhanced body was invulnerable to most damage and he hardly noticed when his feet hit glass rather than pavement, but his lungs constricted in fear as he thought of the destruction he was fated to unleash on the empty city. Everyone had been evacuated but there was still the chance that someone was left, someone who wouldn't even have time to wonder about the sudden flash of light before the nuclear blast incinerated them. The diamond material sheathing his entire body glittered darkly in the sunlight as he neared the encampment. Twenty soldiers and nationalists; the only humans allowed to be in London. Most were well below the nuclear shield, but one man waited at the entrance to the bunker.

The man's already pale skin was ashen as Medane stopped in front of him.

"Plan A," Medane said in as calm a voice as he could manage, "has failed. I request permission to obtain Plan B."

Plan B lay on the ground near the two of them, a deceptively harmless sphere of metal. World governments had first created 'suitcase nukes' in an effort to prevent terrorism. But despite the small physical size, each bomb weighed several hundred pounds and could not be smuggled easily. The detonator was separate, and the man paused before giving him the small metal device that would trigger the seemingly innocent sphere next to them. Medane wondered if the man was regretting the decision to place one of the world's most powerful weapons in the hands of a nonhuman.

"Permission granted. Shelter will be secured in ten minutes."

Medane watched him scurry through the door. Technically it only took five minutes to completely secure the underground bunker from nuclear attack, but Medane knew the humans didn't trust him as much as they claimed.

He lifted the nuclear bomb in one hand. It was barely bigger than the basketballs he and the two other díamonts had played with years ago, in human form, of course, since playing while protected by their virtually invincible diamond skin wouldn't be a challenge. Medane tucked the bomb under his arm, carefully held the detonator, and started running back to the city. The closer he got the bomb to Soren, the rogue díamont, before detonating it, the better. The díamonts couldn't be killed, but the nuclear blast would disable them. It would also disable Medane and his friend Atheus, both of whom were working with the nationalists to stop Soren from destroying the planet. The government assured them that they would not be destroyed along with Soren, but Medane knew they didn't care about his life. He had no illusions about his future. The three of them would be kept unconscious until the government found a way to destroy them. The friendship and gratitude the humans constantly professed to Medane was simply a way to make sure he and Atheus didn't turn against their creators the same way Soren had.

Medane slowed as he approached the sounds of shattering glass and falling brick, the only sounds of life in the city. He followed the sounds until he saw the two díamonts outlined against the blackened brick buildings. Atheus was safe, Medane noticed, and he glanced up as Medane approached. Despite their dire situation, Medane smiled at his friend. He wanted to greet him with a hug and pretend that nothing else was going on, but he knew that Atheus would never forgive him if he failed to detonate the bomb. Atheus, a human figure whose outlines were blurred by blood-red diamond, had been the first to recognize that wearing their díamont form made them immune to human emotions such as pity and sympathy. Only by remaining in their weak, vulnerable human form could they remain human. The longer the diamond isolated them, the easier it became to view the humans as destructive pests and nothing more.

He and Atheus made eye contact and Medane saw his own doubts about their fate reflected. He longed to reassure his friend that the humans would keep their word and allow the two díamonts to live, but before he could speak, Soren slammed into Atheus, knocking him to the ground.

Medane knew he needed to act now, before Soren did any more harm. But as he looked at the two díamonts, he understood that the kinship he felt with them could never happen with a human. He belonged with the díamonts, not the humans. Medane had been in díamont form for nearly three months, now, and was beginning to forget what it felt like to be human. What had the humans done to deserve his trust? Did he have the right to destroy himself and his brothers?

Soren looked like a sinister angel perched over Atheus, light from the sun sparkling against his snow-white body. Soren's mouth was moving as he whispered something to Atheus, trapped under him on the ground.

Soren used words as poison to twist minds to his will. He had manipulated religion in order to convince the humans to overthrow their governments and take control of the planet. Only Medane and Atheus had refused to listen to his eerily seductive and reasonable arguments. He lowered the bomb and stared at his friends and brothers, the only other díamonts who would ever exist. Then, he swung his arm and tossed the bomb towards Soren, who instinctively caught the flying object the same way he had caught the basketball when they were kids. Medane closed his eyes and squeezed the detonator.

CHAPTER 1

Fire flickered at the edges of the horizon as the sun ascended into a layer of smog. Streams of light reached the spires of the city, reflecting against the crystalline skyscrapers as a field of daggers over a bleak horizon. Winds whipped through the towers, carrying voices upwards from the pedestrian walkways circling the major buildings of the city where thousands of people massed and surged. The crowd crept along, seeking the heart of the downtown, a black tower dripping blood as the red sun glistened against its windows. Nalia remained at the center of the crowd for now, enjoying a rush of adrenaline as she listened to the crowd she had organized. This was the biggest protest in decades and Nalia's heart swelled with love and pride as she watched her people, her protestors, follow her plan and march against the government.

The protestors massed on the walkways and flooded out of the slums towards NeoLondon's financial district. Some carried guns, but most held only signs and a hope for peaceful resolution. All wore the bright clothing of the lower class, a vivid contrast to the wall of gray police preventing them from entering the district. The protestors gathered on the 30th floor walkway near three of the largest banks in the United Eastern World. Some of them worked at the banks, mopping floors, filing papers, doing the tasks too menial for the upper class to undertake and too unimportant to replace with robots. Some of them were happy at their jobs and might have exchanged greetings with their pastel-clothed superiors in the lobbies before the start of today's workday if they weren't marching. Others had red tags on their personnel files marking them as 'only suitable for midnight shifts.' The government provided jobs to everyone who requested one, but carefully watched those who did not appreciate this generosity.

This was the first time Nalia was leading a protest, and already it was larger and better organized than any in eleven years, ever since the Graveyard Massacre in 2124 CE. It wasn't only because of her influence that the people were gathering; the United Eastern World was considering officially adopting the secular religion called Kaonism that already ruled most of the planet. Almost everyone followed Kaonism in their personal lives, but many objected to its use in law. The new laws would mean restrictions on all aspects of life, from birthing rights to criminal courts, but the current laws prevented her people from having any representation in government so rioting was the only way to express their outrage.

Still, as Nalia marched with her friends and followers, it was nice to think that she was the true cause. After all, never before had the resistance movement been armed with someone as deadly as she was. Nalia had first discovered her ability to transform into a díamont two years ago, but at her father's request had never revealed this ability until a week ago, when she began planning the march. This was her grand entrance as a díamont, as someone powerful enough to seriously challenge the United Eastern World.

Impoverished districts had been denied the vote in an effort to discourage people from living there, but nearly twenty thousand people called the slum districts home and the time had come to demand their rights. Eleven years ago, a group of militant protestors almost won the right to vote for citizens of the slum districts of NeoLondon. They had been killed in the Graveyard Massacre, but perhaps a díamont could succeed where humans had failed. The problem was larger than NeoLondon; districts could be categorized as 'slums' and have their voting rights revoked throughout the entire Eastern World. She was glad that the hour of their greatest need coincided with her first appearance as the leader of the movement, and she hoped the government finally paid attention.

The air on the 30th floor walkway sizzled as the sun pierced the sparse cloud covering to bounce against black concrete. Extended exposure to the sun's radiation was strongly discouraged by both world governments, but not yet illegal except along the equator. NeoLondon wasn't as dangerous as the southern cities, but Nalia had advised everyone to come prepared with layers of clothing to prevent radiation sickness or sunstroke. Summer had come early this year, and NeoLondon was known for its blistering summers and foggy winters alike. The marchers were covered yet cool even in the haze. Any discarded clothing was slowly kicked to the outsides of the walkway like shattered shards of a rainbow.

The police sweated in their dark uniforms and probably hoped that the protest would end soon. Both sides waited for something to happen to break the impasse. The protestors had the right to remain as long as they were peaceful, and the police were required to stand guard until they dispersed. Nalia knew that secretly many of the police sympathized with the protestors. Most of the police volunteers came from the lower class and the new laws affected them as much as the protestors. But even the most sympathetic officer must have begun to hate the crowd as the sun rose higher and fell onto the walkway directly.

Nalia took a deep breath and prepared to transform. She didn't think she would ever get used to the shock that ran through her body, or the momentary fear of paralysis before the rigid diamond shell over her skin loosened and allowed her to move. It was terrifying, but for once Nalia didn't mind. This was her moment. She rehearsed what would happen as she began moving to the front of the crowd. The police would be stunned, of course. They would have no idea that another díamont existed in the Eastern World. Hopefully they would call Medane for backup. He was the Eastern World's greatest weapon: their díamont. Nalia would face him proudly with her people behind her and give her demands. She would introduce herself as the new leader of the movement and announce the name she had carefully chosen as her public name.

Nalia knew that she needed a false name in case her enemies tried to locate her, and she had chosen the last name of her namesake from sixty years ago: Galley. The name came from an obscure freedom fighter before the Last War. Nalia Galley had successfully ousted a corrupt government and had just begun reforms when the Last War broke out. The chances of any government employees knowing about her namesake and connecting her to the díamont named Galley were slim. Nalia took a deep breath and stepped forward as Galley, trying to adopt the cool, collected exterior she had carefully prepared.

A murmur ran through the protestors and they began shifting to let Galley through. The police gripped their stunguns tightly. She could barely breathe in the thick anticipation surrounding her. This was the first time many of them had seen her as Galley and she knew it was a shock. Galley was like them, born to human parents, but she had the same genetic enhancements that gave the government such powerful weapons. A díamont who served the people, not the establishment.

She could feel everyone's eyes on her as she stepped into the empty space between protestors and police. They were watching her, judging her, comparing her to the díamonts of legend. She was not as tall as Medane or Atheus, the two surviving díamonts. Her skin was covered in opaque sapphire material, hard as diamond and impossible to damage. Galley had never considered that she might frighten her own people, but they were watching her with strong fear mixed with pride. Did they worry that she would turn against them and become like the other díamonts, a stooge for an immoral government? They had nothing to worry about. She would fight for her people and she would die for them, and she would use the strange genetic gifts she had been born with to finally force the world to see what injustices were being done.

She said nothing, simply stood and waited at the front of the crowd while the police made frantic calls requesting backup. Hopefully her appearance would force Medane to show up. He was her main target— not to kill, since díamonts couldn't be killed, but if she could disable him or weaken him, perhaps the government would listen.

In minutes, a single airship circled into view around the buildings and descended rapidly. The protestors edged back but Galley didn't flinch as the ship landed less than ten feet away. She couldn't afford any weakness at this most important moment. One figure emerged, and the protestors let out a gasp of astonishment when they saw the black diamond covering the man's form. Medane, one of the díamonts who survived the Last War. Although he never fought against humans directly, everyone knew that Medane was the real power in the United Eastern World.

He was nearly a head taller than she, Galley realized in surprise. She hadn't been expecting that big a difference and she hoped she didn't seem diminutive in any way. His body was hidden by rich black diamond, the color preferred by elite military figures. His face and any details about his body were masked behind the diamond and she knew her identity was protected as well. As a díamont she couldn't be harmed, but she spent most of her time in human form, vulnerable to attack. She knew Medane was observing her as well and found herself standing up straighter.

"Who are you?"

Medane spoke first, words clear but voice muffled. It was impossible to tell if he was surprised by the new díamont, or threatened, or if he was preparing to annihilate everyone. He was inhumane, robotic, deadly.

"My name is Galley," she announced. Her voice was strong and defiant, unlike the flat tone of the other. "We demand that the Kaonite laws be revoked."

The protestors half-heartedly cheered because this was what they believed, but perhaps hearing it said in the strange voice of a díamont weakened the message because the cheering was not as enthusiastic as Galley would have liked.

"Our political system is designed to accommodate reasonable objections."

"The political system is designed to prevent our voices from being heard. We are tired of being told the same pacifying lies while you sell our justice system to the highest bidder. We demand a voice in government!"

The protestors were more sincere this time and Galley nearly smiled. They were accepting her as their leader even in her díamont form. Medane would have to listen. One protestor raised his gun into the air to emphasize his passion. One police officer snapped his stungun into posi-tion and fired. The protest exploded.

Galley winced as the rows of police started firing into the crowd. No one would be killed by the stunguns, she knew, but she had been caught by a stungun once and still remembered the pain and shock vividly. She kept her face smooth and impassive, though, so Medane wouldn't see her concern. He barely seemed to notice the increased activity around them. She wondered if she looked as inhuman and untouchable as he did. She needed him to see her as a serious threat, but she also wanted her people to know that she cared about them.

A woman's scream pierced the air and Galley stepped forward. "Stop this."

Medane said nothing.

"Order your people to stop," Galley said.

Medane lifted a hand and a few officers stopped firing, but by now the crowd was returning fire and the police were under attack. Medane watched her as if curious to see what she would do.

Galley lunged and landed a punch on Medane's stomach before he could defend himself. Sparks flew as her diamond fist smashed into his diamond torso. She knew he could feel pain even if there were no phys-ical marks on his body and she started swinging wildly, desperate to hurt him as much as his men were hurting her people. He was quick and spun away from her fists no matter how hard she tried to strike him. The only sounds she heard were her heavy breathing and his; protestors and police alike stopped to watch the díamonts battle. At least her people wouldn't be hurt anymore, she thought as she braced herself. She needed to keep Medane distracted long enough for her people to get to safety, but they seemed more interested in watching than running for safety.

After managing to put a few feet between herself and Medane, she gestured for her people to leave. Some obeyed. Medane's police made no move to stop them. Galley circled nervously, wondering what Medane was waiting for. Too late, she realized she was circling until her back was against the edge of the walkway. He shoved her against the railing. Through the railing. She fell.

Galley dug her fingers into the concrete building and slowed. If there had been windows or glass instead of concrete, she would have fallen the full thirty stories. As it was, she skidded down several stories, leaving deep gashes in the pale building. She needed to get back to protect her people.

She carefully made her way towards the nearest walkway, aware of Medane watching her progress from above and shouting at his people. As soon as her feet hit solid ground and she was out of sight, she turned back into her normal human form and headed for the closest building. She made it to a lobby full of panicked protestors just as the police arrived, and raced out to the walkway. She blended into the crowd and slowly climbed the steps up to the 30th floor, fighting against the fleeing crowd every step of the way. Nalia was the leader; she needed to make sure everyone was safe before she could leave.

Just as she exited the building and returned to the walkway, she heard a thin whistle and looked up. Medane stood only a few feet away, she realized with shock, but he didn't recognize her without the diamond shield over her face. The whistle grew louder until it became a shape in the air, plummeting to the earth and landing with a crash directly between her and Medane. Surprisingly, it didn't pierce the walkway but instead lay on the slightly dented asphalt. It didn't even look damaged. Medane was startled and two protestors took advantage of his surprise to tackle him. Nalia lifted the object—a beautiful, delicate-looking bracelet—before gathering the remaining protestors together and leaving the area.

She couldn't help smiling as she glanced back and saw Medane and the police in complete disarray. The protest might not have been entirely successful but she—as Galley—had proved herself a capable leader of the movement.

MEDANE BARELY WAITED for the protestors to leave before returning to his office and summoning his fellow díamonts Atheus and Lethe to an emergency meeting. Both lived in the Western World and Medane worried the entire four hours it took for them to arrive. They wouldn't be traveling together, Medane knew, and when they arrived it would be the first time in years the three living díamonts would be in the same room at the same time.

Only there weren't just three of them anymore, Medane thought angrily. A new díamont. It shouldn't be possible. It meant that all of his suspicions about Atheus were true. Why would Atheus deliberately violate the law against creating new díamonts? He above all people knew how dangerous a rogue díamont could be. Or he should. Medane and Atheus had been the only ones to stand up to Soren during the Last War and they had vowed never to allow that kind of destruction to happen again.

A light flickered above his desk and Medane tried to compose himself. Atheus had arrived. He had just released a deep breath when the elevator opened and Medane saw Atheus through the glass door as the assistant showed him in. Lethe wouldn't be far behind.

At the sight of Atheus' balding, pale head and lightly wrinkled face, Medane's anger softened. He remembered the nights they had spent together huddled in a military base, wondering if the humans planned on executing them. For so many years, they only had each other as friends, and it was hard to sustain any real anger in the face of such friendship. Atheus' face lit into a sincere smile, and Medane clasped his hand.

"My friend," he whispered.

Another flickering light went on and both men paled. Lethe had arrived. Friendship vanished, replaced by resentment and fear. Only one creature on the planet had the power to destroy díamonts: Lethe. Lethe was a díamont himself, but almost never wore his díamont form or used his powers. He was created solely for the purpose of killing Soren, Medane, and Atheus. Once that task was accomplished, he would kill himself. When Lethe first woke up in the lab, Medane and Atheus had been prepared to sacrifice their lives if it meant an end to the violence. They took care of Lethe during his brief childhood, and when it was Lethe's time to kill them, he had refused. Instead, Lethe said that they could continue to live as long as both of them maintained peace in the world.

By calling this meeting, Medane knew he was signaling an end to the era of díamonts. Atheus had crossed the line by creating a new díamont, and both of them would pay the price. Looking at Atheus, Medane wondered why he had done something so reckless. Atheus must have had his reasons for creating a díamont, Medane reasoned. Perhaps it was wrong to assume that his motives were evil. Medane should at least give his friend a chance to explain himself.

The three men stood until Medane realized they were waiting for him to start the meeting. He gestured them to sit, trying to hide his awkwardness. He was a world leader and knew how to command people, but in his heart he still thought of Atheus as his older brother and Lethe as his boss. It was strange to be the one leading the meeting when he held them in such high regard.

"Thank you for coming immediately," Medane began.

He paused, trying to figure out a way to introduce the subject without laying blame on Atheus. He must have paused too long because Lethe leaned forward and spoke.

"I know none of us likes being together, so let's make it quick. Why are we here?"

Lethe's face was expressionless, but it had been designed that way. Medane knew he was deeply troubled that Medane had taken the extraordinary step of calling them together.

"There's a new díamont in NeoLondon."

Silence. Medane immediately looked to Atheus, who was pale and perhaps even frightened. But was he guilty? Medane couldn't tell.

"The díamont calls himself Galley. He showed up a few hours ago leading a protest. He shows violent tendencies and already has command of a large group of people."

Lethe seemed lost in thought and Atheus refused to meet Medane's gaze. After a long pause, Lethe crossed his hands and leaned back in his chair. Medane and Atheus turned to look at him and Medane knew Atheus was filled with as much fear as he was. Lethe's pale brown skin matched his pale eyes perfectly, and his face was sculpted perfection. He had not aged at all since first opening his eyes forty-nine years ago.

"The new díamont must be primarily human," Lethe said. "I would know if another true díamont had been created. I can destroy díamonts." Lethe lifted his hand as if in illustration and Medane and Atheus flinched. "I can weaken this new díamont and prevent him from becoming a díamont, but I do not kill humans."

"So you can make this threat human again, and we can destroy it?" Atheus asked.

Lethe nodded. Atheus appeared relieved, probably because no mention had been made of finding out who created the díamont in the first place. Medane wondered if creating primarily human díamonts violated any of the carefully constructed treaties. Lethe was designed to implement all of the treaties, so he would know better than anyone if a law had been broken.

"Thank you," Medane said. "I have someone—a human—who I believe can infiltrate the resistance movement and locate the díamont. Once we find out who the díamont is, I can bring him to you."

"With all due respect, Medane," Atheus said with a sneer, "I doubt a human of yours will be able to handle a díamont."

Medane nearly smiled. Now that Atheus' fear about being caught by Lethe had vanished, the arrogant bastard was already trying to take over the meeting and the mission. Normally Medane would yield and let Atheus lead, but if Atheus really were the creator of the díamont, then it was probable that the díamont would vanish before Lethe could destroy it.

"My human has a much better understanding of my country than any Westerner would," Medane said. "I have complete faith in him."

"How long will it take?" Lethe asked.

"A week."

Medane hoped that was the truth. The human in question, a former resistance fighter who called himself Raven, had a fierce independent streak and had vanished two days ago. Not for the first time Medane wondered if he needed to be stricter with him. To Raven, Medane was a boss and nothing more, but to Medane, Raven was almost like a son and the thought of restricting his movement and freedom went against the love and respect Medane had for the man.

"Who is he?"

Atheus' question sounded casual but Medane knew what he was asking. Atheus may or may not have been trying to create díamonts, but it was no secret that Atheus had led a research team devoted to breeding superhumans.

The project had been around for nearly a hundred years before Atheus took it over, and Atheus had hoped to create an extremely powerful army with the breeding subjects. Medane had assisted, in the hope that the army would be used for peacekeeping. Even Lethe had allowed the project to continue until a plague killed nearly all of the subjects. Lethe officially closed the project, but Atheus gathered the few survivors to see if one more generation would create the perfect balance between strength and adaptability. Two children were born, as genetically different as humanly possible yet both possessing incredible strength, speed, and stamina. One of the children, the boy, vanished around age six. Atheus always accused Medane of kidnapping the boy. Medane never directly denied it. He viewed it as saving the boy's life; Atheus saw it as theft. This was the real question Atheus was asking, and for the first time, Medane acknowledged Raven's true identity.

"My human goes by Raven, and he is a product of the superhuman research."

Atheus' eyes narrowed and he was about to speak when Lethe lifted his hand. "There is also the question of how the díamont was created."

Fearful silence fell as Lethe studied both of them. "Medane will find the rogue díamont and bring him to me. I will wait until then to decide whether or not any laws have been violated. Until then, I will be at the embassy. Atheus, I expect you to remain in NeoLondon until I have made my decision."

Medane let out a sigh and stood, showing the two men out without another word. Atheus glared at him but didn't dare speak in front of Lethe. At least they would have time to understand the new threat before their lives would end.

CHAPTER 2

Only a sliver of the Earth was lit by sunlight in the moon colony's observation deck and Kaela took a few minutes to admire the sight before continuing her patrol of the science stations. The dark phase would begin in a few hours; two weeks of the moon colony facing away from the sun. Most tourists left during this phase, but Kaela thought it was the most beautiful time in space. Without the sun's glare, stars were brilliantly visible and the Earth glowed with reflected light.

Kaela often stared at her planet and traced the outlines of the Pacific coast in the privacy of her room. She didn't want anyone to know how much she missed her life on Earth. Her boss Atheus had given her a pardon and a new life here and she couldn't appear ungrateful, but she had spent the last eight years trapped here and she missed being surrounded by new people and fresh air.

Kaela began her rounds without thinking, checking in each lab as she passed, nodding at the familiar faces inside and giving them tacit permission to continue whatever illegal operations they were conducting. She exchanged smiles with a doctor who had been smuggled off Earth after publicly commending Nazi research techniques in the Second War. She didn't know what he did here but secretly she hoped his statement had been taken out of context and he was trying to find cures for recent super viruses. She knew this was a false hope. The whole reason Atheus had built the moon colony was to give science a place to develop without ethical or moral boundaries or laws.

The lower security areas were clear, as usual. There was no reason any tourist would want to visit and very few ways to end up here by accident. The only danger was that a reporter from the press conference would try to sneak in and gather information. Kaela hated having representatives from the largest news outlets so close to the research centers, but the reporters were easy enough to spot in their dark grey jackets and bright yellow press tags.

The research centers were plain white structures with black windows running from shoulder-height to the ceiling. The entire complex had a uniform design and was unmistakably different than the sprawling spheres that held living quarters and tourist attractions. Kaela paused at the entrance to the high security area, which was distinguished by a slim red line dividing the white wall and black windows. She opened a hidden keypad in the wall and checked for activity. Eighteen people had entered the area in the past six hours and four people had left. Normal numbers for the day before a dark phase, Kaela thought, and slid the cover shut on the keypad.

Even though this area was supposed to be Kaela's primary concern, she spent as little time in the heightened security area as possible. She had been shocked to learn that Atheus' main project on the moon was research on creating and destroying díamonts. It violated the essential terms of the Sydney Accord, negotiated to end the Last War and prevent another. If she told anyone about the research, war would break out, but if the research began producing results, an even worse disaster might occur. It was easiest to let the research continue, Kaela frequently assured herself. Her job was to protect the scientists so that they could study unhindered. Her job was not to make moral judgments on their work.

As Kaela entered the high-security area, she noticed a dark shadow at a nearby intersection. The shadow vanished. She strode forward. If it had been a scientist, he or she probably would have said hello or otherwise acknowledged Kaela's presence. She reached the intersection and saw a man dressed in black, a stark contrast to the white walls. It looked like he was waiting for her. She opened her mouth to ask for credentials but before she could speak, the door in front of him opened and he vanished inside. Her heart thudded. The main server facility for díamont research was behind that door. She lunged with a gasp but the door slid shut and she swore as she quickly typed in the override codes. Whoever he was, he shouldn't have been able to get inside. How did he get the code? Her finger slipped against the slick pad and Kaela took a deep breath and carefully reentered the numbers.

The door slid open and she leapt in without thinking, expecting to see the man in front of her. The chill of a gun against the back of her neck shocked her. This was not a member of the press. He was a real intruder. Stungun or real, she wondered. It felt real, but weapons with bullets were banned after the Last War. The only people who carried such weapons were hired killers who wouldn't hesitate to take a life if it meant their own gain. Kaela had a similar gun in her waistband if she could just get to it.

"Drop your weapon on the floor," he said. His voice was gentle, almost reassuring. He didn't sound like a killer. But stunguns usually weren't this icy cold.

"I'm unarmed."

The lie came to her lips without hesitation. Already she was trying to rationalize his death. Clearly he was a threat; clearly he meant to harm her. Her job was to kill anyone who found out about the díamont research. She would worry about morality later.

The weapon against her neck shifted, but not enough to let her avoid a bullet. His hand rested on her hip and slid forward. For a moment she thought he was going to attack and rob her like the other man had eight years ago, on Earth, threatening her friends and foster family if she resisted. She would not let another man turn her into a victim like that, but she was too frightened by the memory to stop him. She gasped in dismay when his hand slid over her waist to her carefully concealed gun. He took it from the holster and seemed to examine it behind her back before tossing it on the ground a good distance away.

"I'm not here to kill you," he said. "But if you lie again, I won't hesitate."

He pushed her forward against the wall and she leaned against it, grateful for the support it offered her shaking body. Despite the adrenaline surging through her veins, she felt weak and frightened like a child confronted with the reality of death for the first time. She took a deep breath and tried to gather her courage while the man moved away and started entering codes into the access panel of the server. She could just see him from the corner of her eye but she didn't want to move and attract his attention until she had a plan.

He was close to her height and weight and she thought they would be evenly matched if it weren't for the gun. His gun was loose in his hand while he typed but she doubted she could wrestle it away from him. The only way to even the odds was to get her gun. It would take several seconds to duck, slide across the room, and get the weapon cocked and ready to fire. Kaela took a deep breath and mentally envisioned the movements, counting against the rapid heartbeat pounding in her chest and ears. Four seconds if she did everything right.

Kaela inhaled again and rested her forehead against the wall, allowing her to block his view of her face as she watched him. He was keeping a close eye on her; there was no chance of a stealth attack. She needed speed and luck. His left hand tapped against the keys while his right held the gun—a real gun, she silently confirmed. Her fingers trembled and she tensed to prevent a shiver of fear from running over her. Every few seconds he paused, seemed to think for a minute, then returned to typing. Must be bypassing the security. No alarms were sounding so he must be doing an excellent job. Security codes were time-sensitive so if she went for the gun just as he tried entering a code, he might be too distracted to react immediately. It was the only chance she had of getting the advantage and she steeled herself in preparation.

He paused and his eyelids flickered as though he were deep in thought, probably calculating the time since the previous code in order to enter it correctly. Just as his left hand made the first downward strokes on the keyboard, she lunged. Down to floor, grab gun, lift, aim, release safety and fire—nothing. She squeezed again and heard the empty cartridge click, then she stared at the figure in front of her, a target moments ago and now a deadly threat she couldn't fight. He lowered his gun sideways, opening his right hand to show her the bullets in his palm.

"You won't get far without these. Now get up and come here."

Kaela's arm sank into the ground of its own will, and she lay on the floor for a moment, the rush of her successful lunge freezing her in place until the man snapped his hand shut, bullets clinking against the gun handle. She got to her feet. She realized that he now stood between her and the exit. Had he dropped the gun there on purpose, knowing she would dive for it and become trapped? Her teeth clashed angrily and she imagined slamming the gun into his head and wiping what had to be a smirk from his face. The asshole was watching her, smiling, as if he knew exactly what she was thinking.

"Come here," he repeated.

Kaela took two small steps forward and flinched as he grabbed her wrist, tightening until she dropped the gun. Instead of releasing her, he pressed her palm against the keypad. She blinked in shock as the pad turned green and the security system turned off. She didn't have that kind of clearance. He let her go and she stared, watching him start erasing the entire server. He must have manipulated the system to give her complete clearance. She was already in the base records but it should have been impossible for an imposter to alter data like that.

"Don't try anything," he said. He didn't look at her; his gaze was fixed on the computer screen. "I don't want to have to kill you."

His voice was soft against the hum of the computer and the click of keys as he hacked into the central data server. He was good. She had never seen anyone use a computer the way he did. Data flashed across the screen as updates from various scientists appeared and disappeared. He seemed to be reading some, ignoring some, but deleting all and she lifted her hand in a vain attempt to stop him. He ignored her.

Kaela's eyes grew warm and she blinked to keep back tears. Trapped and helpless, again, forced to watch a man destroy the things she was supposed to protect. For nearly ten years she had trained in martial arts and learned how to use every type of legal and illegal weapon she could find, she had forced herself into a life of hard exercise and solitary meditation, she had sacrificed everything to be strong and brave enough to stand up to men and now this man had lured her into the room, tricked her into moving away from the door, used her identity to unlock the computer system, and all without any effort on his part that she could see.

She thought about killing him with bare hands. He would be able to stop her, she was pretty sure, but at least she would die fighting. The man to attack her in the darkness of a decaying suburb of Old Portland had leaned in close to threaten her. He knew her foster parents' names, her best friend's name, and unless she gave him what he wanted, he was going to kill them. Then he grabbed her. Her nails had dug into his throat as she dragged him down and her other hand tore across his face, into the softness above his eyelids, and he screamed as she broke his neck with a sharp twist like she had seen in movies. Only in the movies, the heroine escaped. She was trapped and caught by the police, and would have been sentenced to death under Kaonite laws if Atheus hadn't stepped in and smuggled her to the new moon colony.

Atheus would expect her to kill this intruder, but her hands were paralyzed by the memory of killing and she knew that she wouldn't be able to kill, not without a weapon.

Kaela drew in a shuddering breath as the computer screen faded to black and sparks started to fly from the electronics. The man grabbed her shoulder and pushed her through the doorway into the hall, forcibly steering her towards the nearest emergency exit. She was shocked to see a small airship docked outside. How had that escaped the sensors? A crash from behind them, and the lights went off. The building was black, and the sun was starting to set.

The thought of everyone on the base freezing to death in a powerless, sunless trap snapped Kaela out of her stupor, and she shoved the man's arm away. She landed a solid punch in his gut and knocked the gun out of his hand. He twisted her arm behind her back as the gun slowly settled to the ground. Artificial gravity was off. Kaela flinched as something surrounded her head but it was a helmet, and she was too surprised about being alive to keep fighting as he opened the exit. He should have opened the exit first, then the lack of oxygen would have killed her. But he seemed to want to avoid having to kill her even now.

"The base will be fine," his muffled voice said from behind her. "Life support is still functioning, only the nonvital systems were disabled."

The small airship was two nearly weightless steps from the exit. The man shoved her into the passenger seat. He securely strapped her into the seat and pulled himself to the pilot seat, strapping himself in while starting the takeoff sequence. Less than a minute later, the engine rumbled and her stomach turned. It felt like the pressure of takeoff flung her organs backwards and she shut her eyes and held her breath to stay conscious, but it had been too long since her body had been under this much stress. She blacked out.

RAVEN SET the ship in a gentle descent and checked on the woman. Strong pulse, just knocked out. He probably shouldn't have accelerated so quickly, but he hadn't wanted to take any chances getting off the moon. Raven glanced out the window back towards the dark moon. Scott was there with the rest of the Eastern World press. The real purpose in going to the moon was to visit his friend, since they rarely saw each other outside of work. Scott's wife, Lydia, worked on the moon and Raven hadn't seen her in years. It was supposed to be a purely social visit, a chance to be with people who didn't have ulterior motives for hanging out with him. Raven couldn't remember the last time he had been able to relax with friends. Scott was the only real friend that he had; everyone else just wanted to use him for their own gain.

But when Raven had snuck onto the moon base, he couldn't help taking a look at the classified quadrants. Scott regularly visited Lydia on the moon, but Raven had never been there before. Raven technically had access to the base because of his connection with the government, but Medane had set down very strict rules limiting Raven's authority. Within those limits Raven could do anything—steal, destroy, kill—but if he violated those rules, he was on his own.

Medane had specifically forbidden Raven from going to the moon. Even though both world governments controlled the base, the researchers stationed there were loyal to Atheus, and therefore off limits to Raven. He was taking a chance coming to the moon. If he were caught, Medane wouldn't be able to protect him from the Western World's retaliation. Luckily, though, Raven had not been caught. He was extremely pleased with how easily he had broken into the mainframe, and the woman's appearance had given him the handprint he needed to completely destroy the moon's scientific records. There would be copies and backup data that he hadn't managed to delete, but hopefully Raven had been able to set illegal research back years.

The woman next to him stirred and opened almond-brown eyes. She wasn't beautiful by most standards, but something about her was eerily familiar and he couldn't stop looking at her triangular face, wide nose, and lowered brow. Almost like his, and perhaps that was why she seemed familiar. Taking her was a mistake, he knew. It was impulsive and exactly the type of thing that Scott always said led to all of Raven's problems, but the benefits of getting rid of bad science and rescuing an apparent damsel in distress far outweighed the possible negative conse- quences. At least Raven hoped they did. The moon would only be disabled until the servers were physically destroyed through overheat- ing. Raven had created a temporary inconvenience that would erase years of dangerous scientific advancements and possibly prevent another war.

"Who are you," she asked weakly.

Raven unlocked his safety strap and turned to face her directly. "My name is Raven."

She must have recognized the name because her eyes widened and she was silent. He wondered what rumors she had heard about him. There were a great many out there, and only a few of the rumors were true. Medane started some of the rumors to protect Raven, or so he said, but Raven couldn't see how his reputation as a hired assassin for the United Eastern World could be protection. People knew that he killed and assumed he was a murderer, since Kaonism allowed no other options. No one could understand the calculations and moral ques- tioning that went behind each hit, and no one aside from Medane and Scott realized that Raven's ultimate motivation was to protect as many people as possible.

The woman didn't say anything for a long time, then shrugged as if accepting the inevitable. *She probably thinks that I'm going to kill her,* Raven thought bitterly. *Even though I've done nothing to harm her.*

"I'm Kaela. Did Medane send you?"

"No," Raven said, wondering how she knew Medane. He vaguely

recognized her name. Kaela, one of Atheus' people. Off limits, like every-thing belonging to Atheus. But he hadn't known that at first.

"Then why did you destroy the moon records? Why didn't you kill me? I could see Medane wanting the research destroyed and me off the moon, but why do you care?"

"It… needed to be done."

If she thought Medane had a motive, then Medane might get blamed for Raven's actions. This was exactly why Medane had restricted his movement in the first place, Raven knew. To prevent misunderstandings and potential conflicts that were bound to occur if Raven acted on his own while on the government's payroll. He tried to stay composed and calm. Once he talked to Medane and explained his actions, Medane could come up with some way out of the situation. It wouldn't be the first time Medane had paid the consequences of Raven's impulsiveness.

He looked at Kaela and wondered how she could be so calm. Unless she, like him, was pretending to remain collected while secretly panick-ing. If Atheus interpreted Raven's actions as a direct attack on the Western World—and Raven was starting to consider this as a possibility —then Medane would have no choice but to get rid of Raven. Worst of all, Raven knew that the next time he saw Scott and had to explain why he hadn't stayed for a visit on the moon, Scott would be perfectly justi-fied in saying that Raven's actions were hasty and irresponsible. Scott was always right, and just once Raven wanted to be able to show his friend that he could make good, sound decisions that ended up helping people, not hurting them. But so far, Raven's life was one mistake after another, with Scott and Medane continually picking up the pieces.

CHAPTER 3

Raven's call came at the worst possible time for Medane. Atheus had just sent a message demanding to know why the moon colony wasn't sending regular reports. Atheus had issued various threats and Medane had ignored them, safe in the knowledge that he had nothing to do with whatever was happening on the moon. Until Raven had appeared in his screen with Kaela at his side, contacting him from inner orbit. Medane had cleared them for immediate landing at the capitol building, normally not allowed for outer-atmosphere travel but it would get Raven here quickly.

The ship finally started docking, settling into the sunken heat pad at the top of the government building. Very few ships had clearance here, since it was so close to the President's office. Medane waited while the jets steamed and shut off, and the gate opened. He watched Raven help Kaela off and thought perhaps it wasn't just politeness that inspired Raven to let Kaela go first. Medane knew from Raven's slow walk and lowered head that he was fully aware of the trouble he had caused by going to the moon. But when Raven and Kaela faced him, Raven met his gaze without a trace of repentance. Medane had to hide a smile and focused his attention on the girl.

The two looked remarkably similar, both being the result of a centuries-old breeding project. Though they weren't related, they had both been selected for intelligence, speed, and strength, and these traits tended to be associated with certain physical characteristics. They both had black hair and light brown eyes, skin a muted chocolate, darker than most Western World residents but normal for the Eastern World, where assimilation hadn't eradicated racial differences yet. Kaela was just about a month younger than Raven and the two had known each other as small children, though it was highly unlikely either remembered. Both had had extremely traumatic childhoods and Medane knew that Raven at least had blocked most of his early memories.

"Medane," Raven said, "this is—"

"Kaela. I know."

Medane remained silent and knew that Raven must be worried. The girl glanced between them uncomfortably. It was out of respect for her that Medane finally turned and led them back to his office. She wasn't to blame for Raven's actions and once Atheus found out what she had allowed to happen to the moon base, she would likely be killed.

As soon as they reached the privacy of Medane's personal office, some of Raven's calm exterior cracked and he grabbed Medane's arm.

"I know this looks bad, but I was acting on my own and I'll take any blame for it."

"Yes," Medane said, meeting the other man's gaze before removing his hand. "You will."

Raven visibly gulped and glanced at the girl, who was alternating between watching them and staring out the window. Medane's office faced Díamont Crater, the place where the final bomb of the Last War had decimated the city. Medane had chosen NeoLondon as the capital of the United Eastern World for personal as well as political reasons. It was the site of the last battle of the Last War, the place where Medane had deliberately set off a nuclear weapon in order to stop Soren. He wanted to remember the strife and sacrifice of those days so that he would never allow the world to fall into a similar conflict.

Seoul was the most logical choice to have the Eastern World's capital, not NeoLondon. Seoul had been one of the largest cities in the world before the Last War and it was the only major metropolis that wasn't bombed or attacked. With a population of over 43 million people, it was by far the largest single city in the world. Seoul was also closer to the large Chinese and Indian states, where the majority of the Eastern World's population lived. But when Medane first proposed Seoul as the capital, the European state had refused. They threatened to join the Western World unless the capital were located somewhere in Europe. He and Atheus had agreed that using oceans as borders was the safest way to avoid conflict and Medane could not afford to have a continent split between world governments.

After generous concessions to the Asian state, NeoLondon became the capital. It was not a large city and most of the original city site had been destroyed, but the Europeans were able to accept the choice and the other Eastern states had few qualms. Much of the East had at one point in history been under the control of old London, but Medane gave each state far more independence and control than the old empire had.

Díamont Crater, monument to the Last War, was nearly a mile wide and water had filled much of it to create Lake Thames. Locks built at the start of the century prevented tidal movement and instead of a shore, the remains of destroyed buildings surrounded the lake. The area was preserved as a global monument to the Last War, a reminder of evil and a warning to future generations. Medane had specifically designed his office to face the crater so that he would never forget the sacrifices he had made to protect the people of Earth. Kaela had probably seen pictures of it, but it was entirely different to see in person the flattened landscape, charred and twisted metal beams and the brackish water at the center.

Raven wasn't looking at the crater; he had lived here for years now. He was waiting for Medane. At the moment, Medane couldn't see a way for these two to survive. Kaela belonged to the Western World and Atheus could do whatever he wanted with her. Once Atheus found out that Raven was responsible, the only way to avoid war was to forfeit the Eastern World's claim to him.

"Why isn't the moon in contact with satellites here?" Medane asked.

"Communication was temporarily disabled," Raven said. He sounded confident, but Medane noticed that his hands were clenched into fists. "The moon will be in contact again at the end of the dark phase."

Medane nodded and allowed himself to relax. Atheus wouldn't know anything for sure for nearly two weeks. Nearly two weeks to figure out how to protect Raven.

"And what did you do on the moon base?"

Raven flushed and glanced at the girl. "I destroyed as much of the immoral research there as I could, sir."

The 'sir' was an interesting choice, as Raven rarely acknowledged Medane as his superior. Raven preferred to think of himself as a free agent who happened to regularly take jobs with the government, and for the most part, Medane didn't try to disillusion him. It was part of the tacit agreement both made when he was hired, and the only way that Medane could get Raven—formerly a leader of the rebellion now being led by the new díamont—to work for the government he had nearly succeeded in toppling.

"Anything involving the creation of díamonts?"

Raven met his eyes as if startled. "There was research on díamonts," he said slowly, casting a glance at the girl.

She was pale, as she should be. She had allowed such research to take place and done nothing to stop it. But he was beginning to see a way out of this situation. If Lethe decided to investigate whether or not Atheus was responsible, the first place he would look would be the moon base. If Raven had already deleted the data, then there would be nothing for Lethe to find. Atheus would probably escape without any blame, thanks to Raven. Medane was sure he could convince Atheus to let Raven live in those circumstances, and possibly Kaela as well. He just needed to spin the story well so that Lethe didn't think that Medane was helping to cover evidence.

"I have a job for you," Medane announced, gesturing to both of them.

Raven seemed to relax, as if he knew that Medane had found a way to get him out of this mess. Kaela watched him warily, but with interest. Medane wondered what had happened to finally drive her into Atheus' employment and hoped she wouldn't try to contact him before Medane could discuss this.

"There's a new díamont in NeoLondon." He ignored their surprise. "I want you to track him down and catch him. He probably spends most of his time in human form. Once you locate him, contact me immediately. His powers can be neutralized, and you will need to kill him."

Raven and Kaela nodded together and Medane paused, looking straight at Raven. They both understood how dangerous a rogue díamont was and Kaela was probably prepared to locate and kill him no matter who he was, but Raven was different. There was even a chance that Raven would know the díamont, and sending his favorite agent into the slums was the last thing Medane wanted to do. But he didn't quite trust Kaela to be capable on her own. He needed Raven.

"The díamont is currently leading the resistance movement in the slums."

Raven drew in a sharp breath.

"He has already led one mass protest that ended in violence and injuries to dozens of police and protestors. He is dangerous," Medane said, keeping his focus on Raven. "He will continue inciting violence. People will be killed if he isn't stopped."

Raven was silent. Medane knew he was weighing the consequences in his head. Raven had led the last serious attempt against the government when nearly fifty of his fellow protestors had been killed in the Graveyard Massacre. Medane wasn't sure if Raven would be willing to risk more deaths if it meant that the movement would finally be successful, and he knew that the longer Raven thought, the more likely he was to refuse.

"Kaela, let us speak in private for a moment."

She left quickly, closing the door with a small thud. His assistant would be outside to prevent her from leaving. Not that she had anywhere to go.

"Medane, this isn't my kind of mission. I'm not just some hitman who kills at random."

"I know," Medane said, trying to sound compassionate. "And if I knew anyone else who were capable of this, I would ask them. But this is a díamont, Raven, a serious threat to the entire world."

He could tell Raven was considering, wavering, and Medane continued. "I'm willing to pay you six billion díons for this, three up front. I believe that's about a third of everything you've earned in the past ten years. This mission is that important."

Raven stared at the ground and Medane tried to think of anything else he could add. But it was dangerous to bribe Raven like this. Best to leave it with money, he reasoned. If he piled too many perks and gifts on, Raven might realize he was being manipulated.

"I'll bring the díamont to you," Raven finally said. "But I can't promise I'll kill him. What do you know so far?"

Medane tried to hide his relief and pleasure, limiting himself to a smile.

"Let's get Kaela back and I'll tell you everything."

PHYSICAL LABOR WAS NOT something Nalia enjoyed, but manual gardening was one of the trademarks of the resistance and it was her job to take care of the garden behind her father's business. They were trying to show the government that people were capable of being self-sufficient without worldwide commerce. In many parts of the Eastern World, people used only what they could produce. Nalia had never been to a rural area, but she had met actual farmers from the African state who lived in communities of less than a thousand and had to take fuel cars to reach the city. They were the people her resistance movement was trying to help.

Even though Nalia lived in the slums, she was still a resident of NeoLondon, center of the Eastern World. And when her father had sent her to school outside of the European state in order to broaden her horizons, she had gone to the main center of commerce in the Asian state, Seoul. When Nalia was being honest with herself, she worried that her involvement in the movement was just another elitist attempt to transform the lower class. She had their best interests at heart, but wasn't that exactly what the government said?

Nalia pulled a weed and winced as grains of dirt showered her hands. Her father said that the soil was much better now than it had been just after the war. He had gotten it from the Asian state, where there were still natural areas with no human development, and slowly mixed the rich foreign soil with the ashy native dirt until plants were able to take root. And weeds, Nalia thought as she yanked another out. For every crop that succeeded, there were dozens of weeds. Sometimes Nalia thought her father had called her back from Seoul just to help with the gardening after her mother died.

She dumped the weeds into the incinerator, picked up her basket of vegetables, and headed back inside. Her father said doing daily chores would help her keep in touch with the people despite her new abilities. He said díamonts were only dangerous when they stopped thinking of themselves as human, and he was incredibly strict about how she could use her powers. He didn't, however, know about the bracelet that Nalia had picked up at the protest. The bracelet wasn't made of ordinary metal, Nalia knew, because it had remained intact after being dropped, probably from a passing airship. But it also wasn't ordinary because as soon as she put it on, it seemed to shrink to fit her wrist. She couldn't get it off, but in all fairness she also hadn't tried very hard.

The very first time Nalia found herself trapped in diamond skin and barely able to move, she had been terrified. Her father had talked her through the ordeal and soon she was able to control her body and plan her transition from one form to the other. But she learned very quickly that if she was wearing anything metal when she transformed, it melded with her skin. She had a line of golden skin from her favorite necklace now and was extremely careful about what she wore. But this bracelet remained solid in díamont and human form. Whatever it was, Nalia liked it. She could finally wear jewelry without having to constantly worry about accidentally transforming.

Her father, Klaus, greeted her as she entered the kitchen but didn't look up from his cooking. Their home had long ago been transformed into an inn where homeless locals and resistance fighters gathered for free food and shelter. It was more than an inn in some ways; it was a safehouse where dozens of people could hide in a maze of hidden passages and underground corridors that ran from various secret entrances around the house to ultimately end up in a large bunker deep underground. Klaus had some connection with a European district that let him spend money freely, and his generosity and wealth were the backbone of the resistance. After Nalia's first appearance as Galley, Grader's Inn had been bursting with people from all the nearby islands, and even a few from the main European state.

Nalia emptied her basket of ripe vegetables into the fridge.

"Wash two potatoes, I need them," Klaus said, again without looking.

"They're pretty small."

"Three, then."

She set three potatoes on the counter and finished putting the rest away. She had hoped to get out of the kitchen before being roped into more chores, but no luck. It wasn't that she didn't like helping out, but she wanted to go into the main room, where guests and locals would be waiting to meet her. Not that they knew she was Galley, the díamont, of course. Klaus insisted that she not tell any of the newcomers in case they were spies. Nalia didn't mind. She was still the daughter of Klaus, a major figure in the movement. She still got plenty of attention, and all of the NeoLondoners knew who she was.

The water ran ice cold as she scrubbed the measly potatoes. Hot water was rare in the slums but Klaus usually managed to keep it at a decent temperature. Maybe the government had totally shut down gas pipelines into the slums after the protest. Whatever the reason, the water felt nice after being out in the stuffy and humid garden.

"Peel and slice them, too."

She stifled a groan of annoyance. She knew he was trying to help her adjust to her new fame, but she didn't need to be stuck in the kitchen to do it. Even a year ago, Nalia might have been tempted to throw a fit and leave, maybe even run away to a friend's house before coming home the next day. She was proud of her progress and thought that it showed maturity when she smiled at her father and starting peeling potatoes. She would just have to prove to him that she was ready for responsibility.

Nalia peeled patiently, only interrupting her father to ask how big to slice the potatoes. She had just finished slicing one when there was a knock and one of Klaus' friends appeared at the kitchen door.

"Sorry to disturb you," he said.

Klaus kept stirring, but he turned to face the newcomer and Nalia couldn't help but frown. Her father hadn't looked at her a single time. She had thought maybe he was working on a complicated recipe, but if he could look up at his friend, why not his daughter?

"There's someone new, escaped from the Western World and just made it to NeoLondon. We think she's a member of their resistance league, but no one knows how to tell."

"They use similar codes," Klaus said, the spoon in his hand slowing. "Nalia."

He paused and finally looked at her. She tried to look humble and helpful and everything he would want in a child. She was already resigned to spending the day in the kitchen, stirring soup for hours on end while new people were arriving all the time just down the hall. It was disappointing, but there would be plenty of time to meet everyone. It was important that there be enough food to go around, after all, and as her father often said, the cook is the foundation of any establishment.

"Nalia, I want you to go talk to the newcomer. You know the codes as well as I do, and you've already been a tremendous help in here."

"Really?"

She couldn't help the incredulous smile that sprang to her lips. She did manage to wipe the knife off before dropping it. Klaus smiled at her, the first time in a very long time, and she held her head high as she took off the battered apron she wore when working and glided into the living areas to meet the Westerner.

CHAPTER 4

Kaela tried not to let her experiences in the slums taint her general impression of the Eastern World, but it was hard. This was the first time she had been here and, aside from the government building and a quick ride through downtown, all she had seen were rundown brick buildings and brightly clad peasants. Not peasants, she reminded herself. In the Eastern World, they were known as the lower class. If there was a slang name for them, she had yet to hear it.

Everything about the slums was broken. There wasn't even a functioning walkway—people had to walk at street-level where dust and filth accumulated. The buildings weren't even tall enough to have a walkway, most petering out at five stories. The downtown had been more like a real city, with walkways on the higher levels and transportation on the lower levels, and Kaela had to tell herself that even the Eastern World considered this a slum. She shouldn't be assuming that everywhere in the East looked like this.

Kaela glanced around and made sure no one was watching as she slipped inside a building. Raven had chosen it earlier in the day, saying it was ideal for their headquarters. Since then, she had been out gathering information and meeting the leaders of the movement. She had thought she was discovered when the people at Grader's Inn—which Raven insisted was the main base of the resistance—hadn't asked her any of the coded questions he had coached her on. But after a while a young girl came out, Nalia, and once Nalia accepted her, the rest of the place opened up. She didn't know who Galley was yet, but she had several people she had identified as possibilities.

Kaela opened the door to the small room they would be sharing and stared. Raven had been busy. Three computers were placed around the room, wires running haphazardly between them. One screen looked like it had profile pictures of many of the people she had seen, and another screen showed the room itself as if through her eyes. She looked at Raven in confusion and, out of the corner of her eye, saw the screen shift to Raven as well.

"Camera in the lenses I gave you," he said apologetically. "Picture only, no sound. I know I should have told you, but if you knew about it, you might give it away."

Without a word, Kaela went into the bathroom and removed the contact lenses. She was furious that he had planted a camera on her without her knowledge. He had deeply invaded her privacy and she resented his presumption that she wouldn't be able to act naturally knowing what she looked at was being filmed. He had seen everything she had seen. Kaela flushed, trying to remember what she had looked at.

Raven had given her the lenses because light-brown eyes in a darker-skinned person would seem suspicious to some of the Easterners. He said it had something to do with a propaganda film that came out, and a lack of education in the slums. And she had believed him completely, putting in the contact lenses to darken her eyes without a second thought. She glared at the contacts, now sitting in a small container of liquid, then realized that he could probably see her glaring. She stormed out of the bathroom prepared to yell at him. He was sitting on the floor, busy at a different computer.

"You had no right—" she began, then stopped. He had pulled up profiles of many of the people Kaela had mentally tagged as possible díamonts. Had he been reading her thoughts as well?

"I know. But I've already gotten information on most of the people you met. It's a lot faster this way. Who else looked suspicious?"

Kaela took a breath and tried to relax before sitting next to him and looking at the profiles to see who he had missed. She was upset by the violation of privacy, but he had done it for a good reason and he seemed at least a little apologetic. Plus, it meant that she wouldn't have to retell everything that had happened.

Kaela found the missing subjects and was surprised when Raven discarded some of them immediately. As they talked about her experience and the steps she could take to locate the díamont, she began to wonder about how Raven knew this area so well. And why, after going to such lengths to destroy research on díamonts, he had hesitated when asked to kill the result of that research. She kept trying to get him to talk about something more personal than the job, but had no success until she mentioned that she had told Nalia she was from old Portland.

"Why Portland? I just said to name somewhere in the Western World."

"I'm from Portland," Kaela said. "No need to lie more than necessary."

He was silent and for a brief moment, the mask of smooth composure faded and she saw a young man in torment. She took his hand without thinking.

"What happened in Portland?" she asked softly. Her own memories of the place were not kind, at least her last memories there. His appeared to be no better.

"No, nothing," he said. He shrugged. "It's just—I grew up in Portland too."

"Oh," she said. There didn't seem to be anything else to say, so she stroked his hand comfortingly. His skin was surprising smooth and she fought a sudden urge to tell him everything. He looked so kind and approachable and she knew that he would understand, that he wouldn't condemn her for her actions. She had never spoken about what happened to anyone, even though it still haunted her.

"Something happened to me in Portland," she said, half hoping that he wouldn't hear her, or that he wouldn't want to know more. She must have sounded pathetic because he scooted closer to her on the floor and wrapped his arm around her shoulder. She leaned into him and was grateful for the support.

"I killed someone."

She waited for him to tense and pull away and judge her like everyone else did. He did tense, but his grip tightened around her. He didn't seem too surprised, but then again, he knew that she carried a real gun on the moon base and he knew that she had been prepared to kill him.

"What happened?"

She blinked and looked up at him. His face was full of concern and sympathy, not scorn or condemnation, and she realized that no one had ever looked at her like this before. No one—not even Atheus when he found her at the scene of the murder—had asked *why* she had killed the man. In Kaonite court, motive didn't matter. Murder was murder. She had never been able to explain to anyone that she wasn't a killer, that she had only killed the man because of what he had done, what he'd threatened to do. Despite what she assured Atheus and herself, Kaela knew that she would never be able to kill anyone else. Maybe in the heat of the moment, with adrenaline blotting out her sense of morality, maybe then she could kill someone. But she had met real killers and none of them ever had any sense of wrongdoing. None of them could understand her.

"He attacked me," she whispered. Her eyes were burning and she had to gasp in a breath because her nose was dripping. "He was going to kill my family."

Raven was silent and she shut her eyes. She had never told anyone before. It was almost liberating, like she had finally spoken the words to free herself from a spell of pain and silence. But she still waited for Raven's judgment. Attacks, even paired with death threats, were serious crimes, but didn't earn the death sentence. If he even believed she was attacked. The police who arrived on the scene ignored everything she said, ignored the evidence all around that clearly outlined what had happened. It didn't matter what had happened before she killed him. Murder was the capital crime, and the man, no matter what he'd done, was the victim of murder. Nothing else mattered.

"I'm sorry," he finally whispered. He sounded unsure and she pulled away from his grip to examine his face. Sorrow, compassion, helplessness, but not a trace of blame. "I don't know what to say," he added, as if in explanation of his awkwardness. "I'm sorry."

Kaela's eyes blurred in tears and she hugged him tightly, wrapping her arms around his shoulders and resting her head against his neck. His collar was getting soaked with tears, but he didn't move. He stroked her back and murmured something comforting. Kaela realized that this was the first time she had ever cried about what happened. She mostly tried to ignore it, to run from it. She had never imagined being able to tell someone about it and have them respond like this.

Her tears continued but her lips curled upward, almost into a smile, and she nearly laughed at the joy and relief she felt at having finally been able to properly mourn the girl she had once been before she had taken a life. She held Raven close long after her tears stopped and he never tried to pull away. They had so many other things to be doing and he had so many other concerns than the ancient problems of a woman he had just met, and she couldn't begin to express her gratitude as he gave her as much time as she needed.

RAVEN WATCHED the world through Kaela's eyes the next day. She had put the contacts back in without question before leaving. They hadn't spoken much. Raven still wasn't sure what to say. He couldn't fix what had happened, even though he wanted to. Attacks and threats to family were serious crimes, but while attacks had a clear punishment under Kaonite law, threats didn't. There was no reciprocal action. Murderers were put to death, thieves had property and belongings taken away, and attackers were beaten, but there was no way to determine if a person's threats were serious unless they led to action. Someone accused of threatening to kill someone might be sent to prison if the threat were considered serious enough, but there were no real guidelines.

He wanted to share some of his own past with Kaela, but he still wasn't ready to face what had happened. He wondered if Kaela would be working with him when he was finally ready to stop running from his past and face it the way she had. Probably not. And counting on her would be a mistake. If there was one thing Raven had learned, it was not to depend on other people unless absolutely necessary. Raven had one true friend, Scott, and that was enough. The more people he trusted, the more it would hurt when they inevitably betrayed him.

The rebellion remained remarkably well organized, Raven was pleased to learn. For decades, every capitol in every state had a head-quarters and freely shared information, and communication between the East and West was generally good as well. Yet despite the openness of communication, Kaela was the first government spy to actually infiltrate one of the central headquarters, and she had only managed to do so with Raven's help. The resisters were incredibly loyal to one another and devoted to their cause, and refused to accept anyone who lacked the requisite determination.

The problem with the rebellion was the lack of a clear goal. Raven had attempted to solve this when he led the movement, but looking back, his goals were vague and unrealistic. The general aim was to topple the world governments while leaving state governments intact. They wanted to return to the days of smaller states and nations, when people had different languages and customs based on their location and ancestry. Right now, each state maintained a level of distinction: the Indian state was distinct from the Russian and Asian states even though they were adjacent. But individual liberties and differences were consid-ered less important than world-wide agreement, and minority groups were constantly pushed out of the government because of their unwill-ingness to assimilate into the world-wide norm.

Raven and the other resisters believed that once the world govern-ment had less power and the states had more, the balance of power would again shift to the individual versus the majority. At least, Raven used to believe that. The Graveyard Massacre had shown him the flaw of valuing individual lives. Fifty-two people had been killed. His friends. People who believed in him. Murdered by the police. For the police and the government, the event was entirely a numbers game. A large group of people had threatened the safety of the government and were disposed of. No guilt, no retribution. But to Raven and the handful of survivors, every single death meant an individual person no longer able to live their lives and take care of their friends and families.

Most of the survivors left the movement after that. There was no point risking their lives when the government didn't even notice when those lives were lost. Raven had left as well, and lived with Scott for a few years. Scott was loosely associated with the movement as a member of the press, but he had never been an active member and was firmly against the use of violence to accomplish anything. He was Raven's only real friend and the two of them grew incredibly close after the massacre. When Medane started sending letters to Raven, Scott had destroyed them without telling Raven until much later. Raven was grateful; he wouldn't have been able to handle a message from the corrupt government at first. But eventually he began to see the world the way everyone else seemed to, and he began to accept that a certain number of people had to be sacrificed in order to protect the whole. It wasn't right, and Raven had never gotten used to it, but he had learned to live in a world that had no regard for individual lives.

A message blinked on one of the screens and Raven switched it to communication. It was Medane, and he looked furious.

"Atheus has decided to help lure Galley out by attacking," Medane said. "Make sure he doesn't cause any damage."

"Atheus or Galley?"

"Both," Medane snapped.

His eyes were narrowed to slits and he looked angrier than Raven had ever seen. Raven agreed and ended the communication, glad to be away from Medane's wrath. Especially since Raven knew he was to blame for it.

There was no direct way to alert Kaela of the imminent attack since all communication devices were blocked at Grader's house. Inn, Raven corrected himself. He still couldn't believe that Klaus, one of the least in-touch members of the movement, had taken over after Raven left. But Raven had personally set up the security at his house and it was superb. The cameras in Kaela's lenses had been a gamble, since there was a good chance that the signal would be blocked as well as audio signals. He looked at the screen showing Kaela's field of vision and noticed movement among the people at the back. It took a few moments before Kaela looked up, then stood up and started moving with everyone.

They must have been heading out to stop Atheus, or going to support Galley. Kaela's gaze was flickering between faces too fast for Raven to watch and he stopped, hoping she at least saw something useful. She kept scanning the crowd until Galley appeared, seemingly out of nowhere. Raven replayed the moments before Galley arrived. Nothing. All of the people in the screen a few seconds earlier were still in screen when Kaela looked back. Raven returned to the live feed and found himself staring at Atheus.

He had never seen Atheus before but recognized him. The crimson díamont. He appeared as dark as Medane but as the sun reflected against him, the diamond shell covering his body gleamed blood red. Atheus was walking down the center of the street, casually slamming his fist into old fuel cars and any buildings within his reach. He wasn't destroying much, just enough to attract attention. Galley faced him and the two of them must have spoken. Raven wished the cameras allowed sound. He had to watch the díamonts' body language to figure out what was being said, and it was almost impossible to deduce anything from their thick, shield-like exteriors.

Atheus sprang forward and Raven flinched, the same as Kaela and everyone else watching. The two started fighting, and Kaela started looking around. It seemed as though she were looking for a place with a better view but he wished she would just focus on the fight. The screen shifted to brick for a few moments, then Kaela was looking down on the díamonts from above. Raven had to admit that it was a much better view and allowed for him to see who was closest to the díamonts.

Raven was busy studying the bystanders, trying to find familiar faces, when a blue blur shot out from Galley's hand and struck Atheus. The crimson díamont fell backwards. Keeping one screen on Kaela's live view, he replayed the scene on another. It was almost as if Galley had shot a laser gun, but there was no sign of a weapon. In the live view, Atheus remained down and Galley collapsed as well. Onlookers immediately swarmed Galley and Raven was willing to bet that Kaela was cursing as the crowd blocked her seemingly excellent vantage point. When people started moving away, Galley was gone.

Raven replayed the scene several times, aware that Kaela was heading back to the Inn. Galley must have transformed into a human right there on the street, and of course the people would protect him. Raven watched the laser again and came to the conclusion that it must have rebounded to hit Galley as well, causing both of them to collapse.

He didn't worry much about Atheus being left there; the díamont was safe enough and wouldn't try another attack after being beaten by a newcomer. Raven didn't know much about Atheus but he knew the díamont was extremely proud and vengeful. Atheus would plot revenge, but not so close to a defeat.

The screen to Raven's right showed Kaela arriving at the Inn and locating Nalia, the woman who had accepted Raven's codes yesterday. Raven had never seen Nalia before but she was clearly a person of power. Smart of Kaela to find her so quickly. He studied Nalia as she talked to Kaela, probably reassuring her that Galley was fine. Nalia was beautiful, with long hazel eyes that were slanted slightly and clear, amber skin. She looked almost like someone from the Asian state, but her hair was a rich mahogany usually found in the West. Her eyes focused on Kaela's, and Raven watched her pupils constrict and her expression change to one of surprise. She had seen the camera. Impossible, but Raven knew it was true.

Nalia backed away and Raven saw her leave the building. Kaela must not have noticed anything because she remained. Raven tapped his fingers against the keyboard, fighting the impulse to leave the building and follow her. If Nalia had seen something, she would blow their cover. Even if she hadn't, perhaps she could be a useful hostage. He checked the gun at his waist and paused as he left the building. He should leave a note for Kaela, but there was no time if he wanted to track down Nalia. If she was going to warn Galley, he needed to stop her fast.

Raven sidled across the rooftops, easily escaping the notice of people on the ground. It was late in the day and the shadows were long, and his dark outfit blended in with the tall pipes and chimneys jutting out of the roofs. He spotted a woman just two blocks from Grader's. She was leaning against the wall and gasping for breath. His mind flashed to Kaela's experience in Portland and he wondered if someone had dared to attack her in the middle of the street. He leapt down without thinking. It was Nalia, and she couldn't seem to catch her breath.

"Are you alright?" he asked, reaching out to take her arm.

In response, her eyes shut and she went limp. He caught her before she hit the ground and checked her pulse. She was cold to the touch with a weak pulse. She needed help. He lifted her up and carefully carried her back to the small room he and Kaela had claimed. It was part of an old, abandoned apartment complex and Raven brought the unconscious woman into an adjacent room. He set her down, then grabbed blankets from his room and bundled her up. She was still breathing and seemed a little warmer. He left her and scouted out the nearby rooms, finding a decrepit mattress and several thick blankets. Raven brought them back and attempted to make the woman comfortable.

She was young, he realized, much younger than he'd thought. He and Kaela had brought quite a lot of supplies and Raven returned to his room to prepare a warm drink. As a precaution, he also grabbed a pair of handcuffs. When the tea was finished, he brought it to the girl. She managed to lift her head and take a sip, and seemed a little more awake. He cuffed her to a sturdy pipe running up the wall. Her eyes closed again and he placed a hand on her forehead. Normal temp, steady pulse.

He heard footsteps behind him and jumped to his feet, drawing his gun on instinct. It was Kaela, staring at him and the woman in confusion. Raven put his gun away and felt his cheeks heating. He tried to explain what had happened, how Nalia had seen something and how he had gone to trail her in case she went to Galley, and how she had collapsed, but his explanation sounded more like after-the-fact rationalizing than a premeditated course of action.

Kaela shrugged when he finished and left without a word. She looked hurt for some reason, but he wasn't sure why. He would have let her know that he was leaving if he had had the time. He wanted to follow Kaela and explain his actions and do something to get rid of the pain in her eyes, but he didn't. Couldn't. Was afraid to, Raven finally admitted to himself. If he shared something personal with Kaela, he knew she would be kind and accepting, everything he needed in a friend. They would become close. Maybe he would even feel safe, the way he had before his parents were killed. But someday she would die, and he would be left alone again. No, Raven thought. He couldn't stand that kind of pain again. He couldn't give in to the temptation to trust Kaela; he needed to keep their relationship distant and professional.

After checking Nalia one last time and reassuring himself that she was recovering, Raven followed Kaela, hoping they could figure out Galley's identity quickly and go their separate ways.

CHAPTER 5

Nalia woke up with a pounding headache. Her mouth was dry and the wrist with her bracelet stung as though it were cutting into her skin. She rubbed her wrist and hesitated as her other arm felt heavy. She opened her eyes and realized that she wasn't at home in her room. She was in a strange place, and there was a metal cuff around her wrist tying her to a pipe in the wall. Her heart pounded and she shuddered at the thought of what would happen if she turned into a díamont like this. The chain, possibly even the pipe, would become extensions of her body the same way her jewelry had when she was younger.

The room was small. Her head was throbbing too much to look around properly but she knew she was still in the slums by the blankets covering her and the peeling walls and exposed pipes. There was probably a window, but the thought of sunlight made her eyes water.

"Drink this," a man's voice said.

He was tall, with a slim build, dressed all in black. Only elite government officials wore black. What was someone like him was doing in the slums? She took the cup he offered. It was warm and felt good against her hands. She sniffed it cautiously. It smelled like tea.

"It's not poisoned," the man added.

Even if it were poisoned, she was prepared to take that risk in order to ease the stuffy cotton feeling in her mouth. She took a sip, and another. It tasted like ordinary tea, not sweet and too strongly brewed for her taste. But hot, and wet. She drank the entire cup and when she finished, her headache was starting to go away. She must have been dehydrated.

That must be the reason she felt so weak when fighting Atheus, Nalia reasoned. She still had no idea what the blue light was or how she managed to attack Atheus with it, but Nalia suspected it had something to do with the bracelet that continued to sting her wrist. It was possible that the bracelet was some kind of weapon, but that didn't explain why she had fainted. Twice, no less. Once at the fight, and she vaguely remembered leaving the Inn and collapsing into the arms of a stranger.

"How do you feel?"

The man sounded concerned and Nalia managed a weak response. She didn't want to believe that she had literally fallen into the arms of her enemy. She was a díamont, far too strong and intelligent to go wandering off alone when she felt so ill. And she remembered something about the new girl, Kaela, something dangerous. It was almost as if she could hear Kaela speaking behind her. Nalia turned her head sharply and her head gave a throbbing reminder of its delicate condition. It *was* Kaela, right in the doorway, talking to the man.

"—talk to you in private?" she was asking.

Kaela and the man left the room and shut the door, giving Nalia a chance to examine her prison. There was a window, and it looked big enough to fit out if she could somehow get the handcuff off. She tugged at the metal handcuff but it fit too snugly. She carefully sat up straight, then hung her legs off the edge of the mattress. She tossed the blankets behind her. At least Kaela and the man had been kind enough to let her rest. Nalia tested her strength by putting a little weight on one foot, then the other. She wasn't strong enough to stand yet. But she would be, and then she could get out of here.

Nalia hadn't liked Kaela from the start, but she would have never guessed that Kaela was working with the government. A camera, Nalia remembered, slapping her palm against her thigh. She had seen a camera hidden in Kaela's eye somehow. And she had left the building and somehow ended up here.

The door opened and the man came back in, alone. She studied him. He didn't look too much older than her and his mouth and eyes had faint creases from smiling. He looked like an intelligent person, someone who might be willing to let her go if he thought she were unimportant. Then he introduced himself as Raven and her heart iced with fear. He said it casually, as if the name had no real meaning, but everyone in the Eastern World knew that Raven was one of the most influential and dangerous people in the government, up there with Medane and the President. His name was especially important to the resistance, however, because there was a rumor that Raven used to be a freedom fighter like them. She had asked her father about it once and he just shook his head. He hadn't denied it, though.

Curiosity overwhelmed her fear. "What are you doing here?" She waved her hand to indicate the entire slums, not just the specific room.

"Looking for someone. You're Nalia, right?"

She nodded. He must be looking for Galley. There was no other reason she could think of that would bring Raven into the slums.

"I guess the government is starting to take us seriously, then," she said, trying to sound proud and nonchalant. Inwardly she was wondering if maybe her father had been right and introducing herself as Galley was a huge mistake.

"Even if the resistance got what it wanted," he said, lifting one eyebrow as if in scorn or amusement, "You wouldn't know what to do with it."

It was a common complaint of the government that the resistance knew what it *didn't* want but was unable to articulate what it did want. And to be fair, that had been a major issue before Nalia took over and set up specific goals and timelines. The introduction of Kaonism helped unify the movement as well; regardless of what people thought about having a united world government that ignored minority voices, no one wanted Kaonite laws put into place.

"We've changed a lot since you were here," she said, watching him closely.

He was surprised but quickly recovered his composure. She couldn't help but feel a little victorious. He had been a resistance fighter, and there was really only one person he could be: the mysterious leader of the movement who had vanished eleven years ago. No one ever talked about him, even though most of the people Nalia knew must have known him. And if he was who she thought he was, there was no way he would kill her.

"I mean," she continued, "your name is Raven now, but that's just a public name, right? To prevent anyone from finding out that you're really Bryce, our movement's greatest leader?"

He went pale and looked away. Perhaps she had gone too far. After all, she didn't know why he had left or why he helped the enemy now. She didn't want him to leave; she needed to keep him talking until she figured out what he wanted and how to talk him into letting her go. He clearly wanted to find Galley, and she couldn't see any reason not to tell him. He would figure it out sooner or later, and he might feel indebted to her if she were honest.

"I know about public and private names," she said. He glanced in her direction, but not at her. "All my life I've been Nalia, but when I became the leader of our movement I needed a new name for protection, so I picked Galley."

Silence. Then he met her gaze. "You're Galley?"

She nodded, suddenly regretting her decision to tell him. She could almost see the calculations whirling through his mind. Raven was the Eastern World's most infamous assassin. Even if he had been sympathetic to her cause once, why had she thought that he would value honesty and not just kill her? Nalia gulped and tugged at her wrist, still securely locked by metal.

"Medane said Galley was male."

Nalia stiffened and had to bite back her initial anger. How like the old díamont to assume she was male just because she had power. Had Medane even looked at her when they met? But she had been protected, she reminded herself. The diamond skin hid her appearance. Maybe it was better that Medane had no idea she was female.

"You're really a díamont?" he asked, and she noticed that he sounded curious more than anything. At least he didn't share his employer's limited view of women.

"I'll show you if you unhook me," she offered with a sweet smile, lifting her wrist.

He just laughed, and she shrugged. She knew it would take more than that to talk him into releasing her. But laughter was good; it meant that he was seeing her as a person and not just as a potential target.

"If you tell me what you want, maybe we can work something out," she said. "I know you're not here to kill me."

She didn't know, but she hoped. And his reaction confirmed that he had no intention of killing her. He nodded.

"My job is to take you—Galley—to Medane. After that, though," he said and glanced at his hands. "You'll probably be killed."

Nalia took a breath and tried to steel herself. Death was something she needed to be prepared for. Her mother had given her life to the cause. Nalia should be honored to do the same. But Raven clearly wasn't looking forward to her death, and perhaps she could still persuade him to release her. A thought flashed across her mind and she spoke without thinking, realizing too late how cruel her strategy was.

"My mother was killed in the Graveyard Massacre fighting for the same things I fight for."

She had hoped to gain sympathy, but as soon as she spoke she remembered that Bryce had been the one to lead the attack and he was in many ways responsible for her mother's death. She wanted sympathy, but if he was in fact Bryce, then this might almost sound like a threat. He didn't look at her and she winced.

"I'm sorry. I just mean it can be noble to die for a cause. I'm not scared of death," she added, more for her own benefit than his.

"Who was your mother?"

"Taurena. My father is Klaus."

He examined her carefully from head to toe. She shifted uncomfortably until he met her gaze again.

"You look nothing like her."

"She rescued me at birth and adopted me."

"From the Western World?"

"Yes," she said, puzzled. She had moved to the East when she was less than a year old and never left. Her mother had been extremely careful to destroy all evidence that they were from the West and no one had ever questioned her nationality before.

"I saw a report," he said, as if in explanation. "From one of the cities near Seattle. A woman gave birth to a díamont but the child died immediately. There was a twin; everyone assumed it died as well. One of the nurses stole the twin's body and vanished. I didn't know Taurena was from the West."

Nalia let her head sink. Her father knew so much about díamonts. Once she had asked him how he knew and he said her mother instructed him. So that both of them could teach Nalia how to survive, she now realized. They knew she would become a díamont, but neither of them had warned her or given any indication that they knew before it happened. After the first time, Klaus had invented some story about genetic drift and how becoming a díamont was possible. Even at the time Nalia suspected that the story was false, and as she learned more about how many decades were spent creating the existing díamonts, she knew that there was no way she just happened to be a díamont. But she would never have guessed that her parents knew and didn't tell her. They deliberately lied. She felt betrayed, angry. She wanted to run home and demand an explanation from Klaus. But she couldn't. She was trapped, and there was a good chance she would never see her father again.

"Medane won't kill you," Raven said suddenly. "And neither will I. He doesn't know that you're Galley, and I see no reason to tell him. I can't let you leave," and he sounded honestly apologetic, "but I won't let you be killed while you're with me."

Nalia sniffed. She tried to feel joy that her plan to win his support had worked, but she couldn't. Maybe she wouldn't be killed now, but how would she ever be able to go home and face her father? If even Klaus lied, then there seemed to be no chance of the people of the world coming together to fight for truth and liberty, as she had always dreamed.

KAELA TRIED to hide her resentment as Raven left the girl's room. There was no reason to be angry with the girl, but Kaela couldn't help but feel that Nalia's presence changed the relationship she hoped to develop with Raven. Kaela had never had many close friends, none since she left Earth, but after talking to Raven last night, she had begun to think that perhaps a relationship wasn't such a bad idea. She hated feeling vulnerable, but he had been so sweet. She had spent the entire day trying to observe everything possible so that she and Raven would have lots to talk about. She had even risked attracting Atheus' notice by climbing to a better vantage point during the fight. And when she returned, brimming with news to share, she had found Raven and Nalia lying together in a bed.

Not really lying together, Kaela admitted. Raven's explanation made sense, and Kaela had even checked the girl's pulse to make sure he was telling the truth. But seeing Raven touch that girl with the same tenderness he had used with Kaela—it was a type of anger Kaela had never known before. She felt weak and foolish for thinking that Raven's kindness was aimed toward her specifically. He hadn't cared about her situation or her emotions, he just treated everyone with compassion. It was a ridiculous thing to hate about someone but Kaela would have preferred it if Raven mistrusted everyone except her, the same way that she mistrusted everyone except him.

"She's fine," Raven said. "Are you?"

Kaela glared. He was too damn nice. "Fine."

He didn't look as though he believed her but she didn't care. They went into their base room and Raven called up several profiles on one of the computer screens.

"I think," he began, then stopped typing.

Raven took her hand and pulled her down until they were sitting next to each other, knees and thighs touching. Kaela was very aware of her heart pounding, and of the fact that she hadn't showered since entering the slums. The peasants rarely showered, but Kaela was used to feeling much cleaner than she currently did. She wondered if Raven noticed. He didn't say anything and she tried to think of some topic other than the girl in the next room.

"Did you know that the East has already put some Kaonite laws into place?" she asked, hoping to draw him into conversation. She felt guilty about her curt response and wondered if that was why he seemed unwilling to talk about whatever was on his mind.

"Nothing's been official," Raven said. "But I wouldn't be surprised if a few got slipped in during the last legislature. Which laws?"

"Child licenses are stricter and you can only get them if your family earns twice the poverty level."

Raven whistled. "No wonder they're protesting. I doubt anyone in the slums makes that much. And most couples here are still used to the idea of two parents raising a child. There were a lot of protests when second mothers and fathers were legally allowed."

"Well, I'd rather have four people raise a healthy, happy child than two people struggle to get by and let their child suffer. That's one of the few laws I like," she said, glancing at him to see if he agreed. She couldn't tell, so she continued. "It just seems wrong to create a new life if you aren't prepared to care for it properly."

"Having enough money doesn't necessarily mean you'll care," Raven said rather sharply. "But I agree," he added. "I've been to places where everyone is starving because there isn't enough food to go around. If there had just been birth controls in place, the population wouldn't be too large for the food supply. You have no idea what it's like to see children dying of starvation all around you when just a little bit of forethought from their parents or the government would have prevented it."

Kaela didn't say anything; she didn't know what it was like. She tucked her arm around Raven's waist and rested her head against his. This was her chance to comfort him the same way that he had helped her. She wanted nothing more than to take care of him and protect him as they sat together. He leaned back and gazed into her eyes.

"I'm not sure I can complete this mission," he said.

His breath was warm against her cheek and they were so close she could see specks of gold in his brown eyes.

"Why not," she murmured, more because she was supposed to ask than because she needed to know the answer.

She already knew. Once the mission was completed, Raven would continue working for Medane in the East and she would have to return to the West, possibly even the moon base. They would be separated and the beautiful thing emerging between them would shrivel. She couldn't bear to think of leaving Raven and returning to ordinary life. Everything was better with him here. She was safe for the first time, and she had someone who cared about her as much as she cared about him. She felt like a child again, knowing that there was someone to catch her and support her no matter what, and she wanted to hold on to that feeling forever.

"The woman, Nalia."

Kaela snapped back to reality and stared at him. He was leaning close, yes, but he wasn't looking at her seductively. He looked more like he wanted her to understand something. Kaela swallowed and nearly choked. She coughed and pounded her chest. He drew away from her and rubbed her back. Again, with no emotion other than concern.

"I think we need to talk to Medane. Nalia needs to return to her people, and I—" he patted her back and shook his head. "I don't think I can do this anymore. Medane will make sure you're safe," he added.

"What do you mean? Where will you go? I could go with you."

Even as Kaela spoke she knew that he would refuse. He had allowed his vulnerabilities to show and now he was closing up, retreating, and she couldn't think of a way to stop him.

"No, you deserve better than to go into hiding with me."

"Nothing in the world sounds better," she said, gripping his arm to show her sincerity.

He shook his head again. "You don't understand."

"What don't I understand? Tell me."

Raven sighed and glanced in the direction of the Nalia girl's room. Kaela dropped his hands abruptly. Was he in love with that girl? After meeting her once? Was that why he didn't want Kaela around? She stood up stiffly and started to leave. As she passed the door, heading somewhere away from Raven, she turned and tried to appear poised and calm when she spoke.

"We will speak to Medane. Tomorrow."

He nodded and almost looked like he was about to follow her, but he remained seated. She exited dramatically, not knowing where she was going but knowing it would be someplace alone.

CHAPTER 6

Medane knew that he was losing Raven as soon as the small group entered the main building. Raven had requested a private meeting in a room near the entrance and hadn't given a reason. He had said that he and Kaela had taken one of the rebels captive and would be bringing her. Medane studied them intently and was aware of Atheus doing the same. He had attempted to prevent Atheus from coming, but Atheus insisted on being a part of everything relating to the díamont hunt.

The moon was still out of communication but Atheus had quickly figured out what had happened and why Kaela was now on Earth. Atheus couldn't officially reprimand the Eastern World until communications resumed; until then, he appeared content to passive aggressively sabotage Medane. Not always so passive, though, Medane thought with a grimace. He hadn't spoken a word to his former friend after Atheus smashed through NeoLondon. Atheus might have had a legitimate reason, but Medane knew he really just wanted to destroy something Medane held dear.

Raven led the group, Kaela behind his right shoulder and the rebel behind his left. He seemed to be protecting both of them and Medane reassessed each woman. Raven had never been able to connect with many people, probably a result of his unusual breeding. He had little in common with the average human alive today. Medane knew that Raven did have at least one close friend, a male, and he also knew that Raven had never been in love. Raven treated love like a disease and did everything in his power to keep from catching it. But his behavior now suggested to Medane that he had developed a close relationship to at least one of the women.

It would be natural to assume that he would fall for Kaela, since they had so much in common. Similar childhoods, similar jobs now. But the rebel girl was truly beautiful and held herself with a mixture of arrogance and fear that was identical to Raven's the first time he and Medane had met. If she were intelligent as well, Medane wouldn't be too surprised if Raven was attracted. Especially to someone who reminded him of one of the relatively happy periods in his life.

Atheus' attention was on the rebel as well, particularly her wrists. One was handcuffed to Raven, the other displayed a thin bracelet. It looked familiar, and after a moment Medane recognized it as the bracelet that had fallen from the sky at his first meeting with Galley. He hadn't seen who picked it up and he wondered why she was wearing it now. The rest of her outfit was simple, typical lower-class clothing. Bright blue denim pants, rough cotton shirt in a slightly darker blue. Thin brown slippers, not the type people usually wore outside. Her hair was loosely tied back with a band and she wore no other jewelry.

"Raven, please explain why you wanted to speak to me in person."

Medane already knew that Raven was leaving. It had always been a matter of time. Raven appreciated his job because it allowed him to protect large numbers of people and eliminate the few who threatened others, but he had never enjoyed the job. Eventually, Medane knew he would want to return to a simpler life. It had been a risk sending Raven back into his old life and home, and even more of a risk to give him so much money for doing it. Raven hated bribery and was extremely loyal; it was natural that this mission would test his commitment to Medane. Medane just hoped he had uncovered the díamont's identity and would be willing to share it.

"Before I speak, I would like your assurance that neither I nor Kaela will be killed or punished for anything that has happened in the past week."

"I can only guarantee your safety, Raven," Medane said, glancing at Atheus.

Atheus was glaring but he seemed pleased for some reason. Medane made a mental note to find out why.

"Kaela will be safe," Atheus said.

Medane noticed Kaela shiver as he spoke and wondered again how Kaela had ended up working for Atheus. It didn't appear to be a friendly relationship and Atheus wasn't above blackmail or even torture to get what he wanted. Atheus hadn't always been so brutal, though, and Medane often found it hard to believe that his childhood friend could do the things Atheus was capable of.

"Medane," Raven began, "I respectfully withdraw from this mission."

Medane nodded and began to think of the other possible ways to locate Galley. Raven was the only person capable of infiltrating the resistance, but there were less delicate ways of finding information. Atheus might insist on keeping Kaela here, but he would probably be content to withdraw as well and leave everything to Medane. That way Atheus would still appear to be helping, but there would be very little chance of anyone finding the rogue díamont, let alone learning who created it. Medane knew Atheus well enough to know how he would rationalize abandoning the rogue díamont to Medane and he wished that Atheus would put his personal prejudices aside for once and do something without personal benefit. Atheus had put the lives of the planet at risk when he created another díamont. Medane thought that he should at least be willing to put his own life on the line to prevent another war. But Atheus had changed in the years since the Last War and no longer valued other lives above his own. Even without the rogue díamont, it was only a matter of time before Lethe would be forced to kill both of the díamonts.

Raven took a deep breath and glanced at the girl to his left, the rebel. He seemed on the verge of speaking and Medane recognized the way Raven held his head high and fists clenched. He was about to do something rash, something that they both knew he would regret. But no matter how many regrets Raven might have, Medane knew that he never changed his mind once he had made a decision.

"I will also be leaving your service. Permanently."

Medane winced and glanced at Atheus. The other díamont had a wicked look in his eyes. If Raven had announced his decision to Medane in private, Medane could have assured his safe evacuation from the city. But with Atheus here, Medane was required to arrest him immediately. Raven was, after all, a known killer.

"Out of respect to your long service, Raven, I'll give you five minutes before I sound the alarm."

It was the most Medane could do and Raven thanked him before vanishing out the door with the rebel. Kaela was left standing alone before the two díamonts. Raven had apparently not told her his decision, because she looked shocked. When Medane signaled the alarm, her shock turned to fear and she looked at Atheus. Medane stepped between the two of them but Atheus pushed him out of the way and grabbed Kaela's arm tightly.

"Don't worry, Medane," he said, sounding almost happy. "I'll keep my word. And I'd be far more concerned about that human of yours than the other díamont."

"He's not going to turn against me."

"Even so," Atheus shrugged. "He's not going to last a week without your protection."

Atheus left with Kaela and Medane watched their figures move across the lobby until the door slid shut and left him alone in the conference room. Atheus was right, Medane knew. Raven had made so many enemies over the years. He had enemies in the government from when he led the resistance, enemies in all of the militias because of his efforts to eliminate warfare in rural areas, and enemies in the Western World because of the murder he had committed as a child. Medane wasn't sure if Raven even remembered the last, but Raven did know that he was not welcome in the West. And with Atheus as an enemy as well, there was very little chance Raven would survive without someone like Medane to protect him.

He would survive, Medane told himself. Raven had survived against longer odds than this, and he would again. And if there were anything Medane could do to help Raven, he would do it.

———

RAVEN OPENED the door of the nearest parked car and shoved Nalia in before climbing in himself, hindered by the cuffs connecting them. He tossed her the key to the handcuffs while running his government authority card through the ignition. It would take a day or two before his access was denied, and it would be weeks before all of his electronic access was blocked. He had built in securities just in case he ever quit, and now he would find out how well they worked.

The car sprang to life and Raven pulled out into the car lane just as police poured from the building. One fired a weapon but Raven was out of range. He ducked down to the underpass, where the police would be less able to track him, and headed towards the slums. His heart pumped against his chest. He had quit. Finally. Gone. But now what would he do?

Nalia had unhooked herself and was buckling her safety belt. Raven unconsciously did the same, steering with one hand while he admired the car he had taken. It was a luxury model, designed for speed and perfect for a getaway. He would need to dump it before leaving the main downtown area but he could enjoy it for the moment. He felt like he was in a state of shock, like the things happening around him weren't quite real. He hadn't planned on leaving Medane. He had planned on withdrawing from the mission. But Medane had accepted the news so silently, as if he already knew Raven's decision. And the way Atheus had looked at Nalia—Raven clenched his fists against the wheel.

He hated leaving Kaela to a man like Atheus, but she at least knew how to deal with him. Atheus' face had been so full of pure malice when he looked at Nalia. Kaela was strong and Raven admired her ability to work for Atheus for so many years. But Nalia was young and innocent. He knew she could accomplish all of the things Raven had spent his life trying to achieve. She had the same drive and passion that he had, but he would make sure she didn't make the same mistakes. If he had just left the mission and not severed all ties to Medane, Atheus would take over and Nalia would eventually be killed. He wasn't going to let that happen.

Raven saw another car parked along the upper car lane and slid to a stop almost directly under it. Nalia followed his instructions without a word and soon they were making a less impressive but still speedy escape. This car had no identification on the window, so Raven drove it all the way into the slums. Even if the owner reported it stolen immediately, it would take days for the police to find the unmarked car. He slowed and parked in front of Grader's Inn without a thought. Adrenaline still rushed through his veins. He felt proud and terrified.

Nalia remained seated.

"This is you," he said as politely as he could.

"I know," she said, blushing. "Would you walk me in?"

He started to refuse, then noticed her trembling hands. He wondered if she were still feeling ill after fainting the day before. She *had* moved slowly when they were switching cars. He got out and walked to her side. He helped her and she squeezed his arm as if in gratitude. She pulled him towards the entrance and he stopped.

"Come on," she said in a pleading voice. "It won't hurt to just come in. Please help me?" she added quietly, as if embarrassed to need help.

Raven stared at the doorway. It was open, as usual, and already the crowd inside had noticed their presence. Raven knew from Kaela that the first floor had been opened into a single room. If he went in there, he was bound to run into someone he knew. Or, worse, the relative of someone he had led to death in the massacre.

Nalia seemed to take his silence for agreement because she walked forward, keeping his arm tightly clutched in hers. Silence fell as they entered. Nalia kept dragging him forward until he was surrounded. He didn't think she was trying to get him killed, but perhaps he had misjudged her.

"Nalia!"

Raven flinched at the sound of the voice and at the sight of the man who rushed forward. Heavy-set and short, Klaus had a head of gray but was otherwise unchanged in eleven years. Klaus stopped in front of the two of them and stared back and forth between them. Nalia kept her grip tight and seemed to be staring at her father defiantly. Not the best strategy with Klaus, Raven knew all too well, but maybe Klaus' daughter could get away with it.

Klaus folded his arms and turned to Raven. "Bryce," he said flatly. "You haven't changed at all."

Raven bit back an angry retort, reminding himself that he was in enemy territory. Of course he had changed. He had changed everything since that day. There was nothing left of the foolish, idealistic child he had once been, the child who led fifty-seven people into certain death and only four of them out. He had been an idiot but he had changed and he would never be like that again. Raven couldn't come up with anything to say and settled instead on the man's name.

"Klaus."

"Father," Nalia said, stepping between them, "Raven has been helping me."

"He only helps himself."

Again Klaus' words stung, mostly because Raven knew they were true. He always wanted to help other people, but no matter Raven did, he seemed to be the only one to profit. Or survive. There was nothing to say; Raven had been the cause of Klaus' wife's death. He deserved far more than a few insults.

"I will be speaking with Raven in private," Nalia announced, clutching his arm. "Please bring us tea."

She again led him through the crowd, this time into the large kitchen at the back. There was a small, private eating area and she pushed Raven into the corner seat before sitting next to him. She was blocking his escape but also ensuring that Klaus couldn't get too close to him, and he wasn't sure how he felt about the situation. He wondered how Kaela was doing. He hadn't planned on leaving her like that, but he thought she could handle the situation. He would wait a while, then get in contact with her again. He hoped she knew that he wasn't abandoning her forever. She still had the chance for a real life, though, and she seemed relatively happy in her work. Raven didn't have the right to take her away from that just because he wanted Kaela to have something different.

Klaus set three cups of tea down and joined them at the table, across from Raven. Nalia attempted a smile but quickly gave up.

"Raven," she began, "Thanks for coming in with me. I promise no one will hurt you while you're here."

She glanced at her father as she spoke but he didn't make any comment.

"Raven isn't with the government anymore," Nalia continued, again speaking mostly to Klaus. "He's independent. And I want to hire him."

Both men looked at her in surprise. Raven spoke first. "Nalia, I'm not joining your cause. I brought you back here but that's it. I'm not going to kill you but that doesn't mean I'll help you."

"You don't have to join. I said I'm hiring you. You don't work for the government, so you're a free agent. I'm making an offer."

"I doubt we could afford someone of Raven's reputation," Klaus said, lingering on the last word in a way that made it clear how much Raven's reputation as an assassin disgusted him. "And I don't know what help he could give us."

"He knows the government, and he knows how to get their attention and actually cause change in the system," Nalia said.

Raven watched the two of them argue over his merits without listening. What she said about being a free agent was true. He hadn't thought of it like that before. Without Medane's protection, his image could be posted in the media and any of his enemies could kill him without retribution. He knew the mortality rates of free agents and any employer was better than none. Looking at Klaus and Nalia bickering, he decided that he could do much worse. At least if he worked for them, he would still be true to his values. And Klaus would never let him forget his past failures, so there was no chance Raven would again make the mistake of thinking he actually had the power to change things.

"I have requirements," Raven said, interrupting the father and daughter. They turned to look at him in surprise. "I won't attack Medane. Any of his people, fine, but not him. And I have the right to refuse any job."

"That sounds fair," Nalia said.

"We can't pay you," Klaus insisted.

"Whatever you give me is fine," Raven said. "I have money."

It was true. He had billions in banks around the world. But he used the money to assist refugees escaping from East to West, or West to East.

His only real personal expenses were electronics, and he had his personal computer with him at all times. Even if Medane froze his accounts, Raven had no real need for money.

Nalia grinned, a victorious and somewhat predatory smile. Raven couldn't help but remember the days when he had talked people into joining the cause, and how overjoyed he always felt when he finally convinced people to listen and help the movement. She was so much like he used to be, only she hadn't fallen in the trap of thinking too highly of herself. He wanted to protect her from that mistake and working for her was an excellent way to do so.

CHAPTER 7

The first rumblings of the landing gear woke Scott up and he glanced around lazily. A ship had finally landed on the moon and returned with passengers. Scott understood why it had taken so long, but was still frustrated. Without communication from the moon, Earth had no way of knowing if a plague had broken out in the colony, or, as Scott's favorite movies always predicted, aliens had made the ridiculous leap through the stars and targeted the moon as the first step toward conquering Earth. Scott felt his lips twitch in a smile at the thought. But no, all that was causing the moon's blackout was something Raven had done, and once a ship finally risked landing, the base was declared safe quickly enough.

Members of the press had priority in returning, and Scott took the first flight to get home. Once aboard, he had fallen asleep almost immediately—he and Lydia had taken advantage of their private vacation and now Scott was worn out and quite pleased. He did need to get back to Earth, though, with a story as big as the moon's blackout unfolding. Normally Raven was kind enough to give Scott a heads up whenever he did anything drastic; Scott had earned a career as a superb reporter because Raven always told him when and where news would be taking place. Scott wouldn't, however, be writing about the moon unless assigned by his editor. Too risky. He didn't want anyone to find out that Raven was involved, and he wasn't too sure how the Western World would react. It was a major story and not reporting it would hurt his career, but he couldn't put his friend at risk for a headline.

The air whistled past as the shuttle descended back into the Earth's atmosphere. Scott held his breath. He hated this part. He knew how rare crashes were, but no matter how many times he traveled back and forth to the moon, he couldn't get rid of his fear that the shuttle would collapse under the pressure of reentry. He wasn't even sure that was how it worked. Maybe they would explode, or the engine would just stop and they would fall to the ground. Scott couldn't shake the feeling that at some point in his life, the shuttle would fail and he would die. As the shuttle leveled out and slowed over NeoLondon, Scott took a breath and felt his body unlock. A drop of sweat ran down his forehead and he realized how tense he had been. He took another deep breath and relaxed. When Lydia had kissed him goodbye a few hours ago, she had assured him that he would be fine. She knew about his fear and he loved her because she never made it seem irrational. She just told him every time that he would be fine. It was almost a command, and, so far, the universe had been obliging.

Lydia had been annoyed that he left so early, but then again, the whole thing had annoyed her. It had taken months for all three of them to arrange to be on the moon at the same time, she said, and there was no way Bryce had a reason for ditching them without warning. Scott had just shrugged. He knew Raven better than anyone and had learned long ago that he had reasons for everything he did. They just weren't always good reasons. Lydia was the only person Raven allowed to call him 'Bryce' and Scott had never been able to figure out why, exactly. Normally Raven hated reminders of the person he had been before the massacre. And he never talked to Lydia about any of it. Raven hadn't even met Lydia until after the massacre when he abandoned the resistance. She had been a friend then, although Scott had to admit that even back then he was hoping to marry her.

Raven—Bryce—moved in with Scott and for months could barely get out of bed. Nothing Scott did or said seemed to help. Bryce was eight years younger than Scott and even though their age difference had never mattered much, it was easy for Scott to fall into a mentoring role and take Bryce under his care. Bryce started to recover from the shock and horror of all the deaths of his close friends as a result of what he saw as his own actions. He still wasn't talking much, or leaving Scott's apartment, but Scott had brought Lydia over for a visit and the two had connected immediately.

Scott had to admit that he had been jealous. Still was, to be really honest. Lydia had only been in training to be a counselor at the time, but her ability to listen must have allowed Raven to open up as he had with no other person. Not even Scott, his best friend. After meeting Lydia once, Raven had resumed some of his ordinary activities and even began doing things independently again, without Scott always at his side. Scott was glad, of course, but it was frustrating that *he* hadn't been the one to help Raven. Lydia and Raven had a close friendship now, but it was limited by time and space—they rarely saw each other now that Lydia was permanently stationed on the moon.

The shuttle signal sounded and the door opened. Safe. Scott unhooked the security mesh from his torso and grabbed his bag. A few of the other passengers looked pale; probably their first trip to the moon, Scott reasoned. Most reporters stayed earthside their whole lives. He shook hands with the ones he knew and walked with them through the docking tunnels into the terminal. There were families waiting for some and the woman to Scott's right was swarmed with children the instant she passed security. She had just started working in Scott's department and showed a lot of promise, and she had been astounded when Scott told her that she could take the lead on the moon blackout.

He waved at her and wondered if she could even see the movement beneath the two kids. He couldn't imagine how she had gotten two child licenses until he saw the man she kissed after the children. Extremely rich, with heavy gold rings and a gray suit that almost looked like velvet. A man like that would have no trouble getting a second license and Scott was surprised that the woman had never shown signs of being wealthy. She was always down-to-earth and comfortable, never dressing ostentatiously or commenting derisively about the lower class the way Scott imagined the really wealthy did.

No one was waiting at the aerostation for Scott, which didn't surprise him. Raven undoubtedly knew that Scott was returning but would never go to such a public place. Instead, Scott pressed the elevator button and boarded with a few of the less wealthy reporters. They got off on the 15th floor, where the carport was, but he kept going to the 11th floor. According to most people, nothing good ever happened below 15, but Scott loved going to the lower levels of the city. It was shaded, for one thing, which he appreciated the minute he stepped onto the walkway and into the summer heat. It was also far less crowded and tended to be populated by a fascinating group of people. Most were intellectuals. They could afford to live on higher levels but didn't. After the Last War, Scott's mother had moved here as a child and she met Scott's father just a few blocks from the aerostation, at the place Scott was heading now.

As Scott turned a corner and saw his destination, he wasn't sure which pleased him more: the sight of the quiet bookstore, shelves brimming with antiquated paper books and smelling of musty wisdom, or the black-clad man sitting at a rusty café table outside standing up to greet him.

Scott and Raven embraced before sitting at the small table outside the bookstore. Patrons of the store stared, but the owner had known Scott since he was a child and had become accustomed to seeing Raven. One woman hurried out at the sight of Raven, glancing back almost guiltily. The only people qualified to wear black were elite military units—essentially spies and assassins. It was different in the Western World under Kaonism, but in the East, each state government had a small force of men and women who were sanctioned killers. In the Lower and Upper African states, they were called militias and there were very few laws governing them. One of the reasons Raven had started working for Medane was to try to impose limits on them and change the system from within, Scott knew. He had been partially successful, but even in NeoLondon black clothing was still associated with murder for most people.

The woman leaving didn't faze Raven; in fact, he seemed more relaxed than Scott had seen him in years. His eyes were bright and there was almost a smile on his lips.

"Are you angry?" Raven finally asked.

"Why would I be angry?" Scott replied. "I just got to spend a full week with the woman of my dreams. Although I do seem to recall that someone else was supposed to be there, yes, now that you mention it, I think I had a friend who was supposed to drop by."

"Scott," Raven began, but Scott waved his hand.

"Don't worry about it. I don't want to know the details. Yet," he added. "Once this is out of the papers I want to hear everything. But not until then."

Raven leaned back in his seat and smiled. Scott realized with a start that he couldn't remember the last time Raven had smiled so openly.

"I quit Medane's service."

Ah, Scott thought. That explained his behavior. Medane had been helpful in getting Raven out of his depression and back on his feet, but the job was wrong for him. Sure, Raven had the chance to help people and regulate armies and help distribute food in starving areas—now that Scott thought about it, the job actually sounded pretty good. But it also involved occasionally killing someone and even when the person clearly deserved death, Scott knew how much Raven struggled.

"Need a place to crash?" Scott offered. He was somewhat relieved when Raven shook his head. Raven was a clean, friendly, but intense roommate who kept odd hours and had a tendency to stir up trouble.

"I was hired by Nalia," he said. "She's the head of the resistance now."

Scott couldn't help his disapproving frown. "You can't go back."

"I'm not back. They hired me. It's different."

Scott considered. Going back to the slums was the last thing he wanted Raven to do. There were too many painful memories there and too many people who blamed Raven for the massacre, including Raven. Scott knew Raven wasn't really to blame. He had been a kid at the time, barely eighteen years old. He had underestimated the government, no one in the movement corrected his mistake, and dozens of people had died. Scott supported the ideals of the resistance—how could he not, with Raven as a friend—but he didn't like their militant and close-minded approach.

"I met someone," Raven said quietly, as though he were aware of Scott's disapproval. "Nalia, the one who hired me. She's really nice."

"Nice?" Scott repeated, raising his eyebrows. He had never heard Raven describe anyone as nice before.

"You know," he said awkwardly. "She believes in the movement but she's intelligent, and she really wants to help people."

Scott stared at his friend. Coming from Raven, those were the highest compliments a person could get. Was he in love? A grin swept across Scott's face and Raven blushed. Well, if Raven was in love, it was more than enough reason to return to the movement. Aside from Scott and Lydia—and possibly Medane, Scott had to admit—Raven had no friends. Scott had attempted to set him up a few times when they were younger, but Raven always held himself aloof. People who couldn't see through Raven's mask thought that he was arrogant, self-centered, and insensitive. Really it was just that Raven hated being vulnerable and pushed people away to prevent getting hurt. Raven had even tried to push Scott away after the massacre, but had seemed grateful that Scott ignored him and refused to let go of the friendship.

"Lydia's mad at you," Scott said in a mock-warning tone. He hoped Raven knew that the change of subject meant that Scott was willing to give Raven's new lifestyle a try. He still had reservations about Raven being in the slums, but he trusted Raven to do what was best for him. Plus, Lydia had made Scott promise that he would yell at Raven for abandoning them. Scott wasn't much for yelling, but he would keep his promise in his own way, just as Lydia would expect.

"How is she? I didn't mean to—"

"No," Scott interrupted. "Don't want to know anything yet."

He hated having to censor their conversation, but Scott believed in journalistic integrity and if Raven told him in black-and-white terms that he caused the blackout, Scott would be unable to lie about it later.

"Lydia's fine. Actually, really good," he added, remembering the passionate nights they had spent between boring press conference meetings. "We're, uh, talking about getting a child license." Scott blushed, delight at the thought of having a child of his own temporarily derailing his plan to scold Raven. "She's coming earthside in a week or two and I will not be held responsible for what she does if you aren't here to see her."

"That's wonderful, Scott. How long is she here?"

"Four days," he explained. "We don't know exactly when. Whenever shuttle traffic is normal again. She has a healthcare seminar at the capitol, it's being rescheduled. Everyone on Earth seems to think the moon has such a superb healthcare system, but really they just have fewer, healthier people. She has to explain the moon's system, anyway, and then a committee will try to adapt it to Earth politics."

"Sounds fun," Raven said with only the slightest hint of irony. "I may have to stop by, then. Just for the seminar, of course," he added with a shine in his eyes. "If I happen to see Lydia, that would be a happy coincidence."

Scott laughed. "And if you don't happen to see Lydia, I foresee an unhappy coincidence in your future."

Raven shared a chuckle. They both knew Lydia would forgive Raven the moment she saw him; she might make threats but she had a soft spot in her heart for him.

"I don't really know what'll be going on, what I'll be doing," Raven continued seriously. "Everything's kind of up in the air and I'm trying to stay under cover for as long as possible. But I'll make sure to see her at least once while she's here."

"Promise?"

Raven hesitated, but Scott had told Lydia that he would get Raven's word. Raven never broke his word. Partly because he almost never gave it.

"I promise," Raven said quietly. "I'll see her."

"Thank you," Scott said. His watch beeped. The office. He had told them he was making a stop before returning to work but they needed him now. Probably needed readers and writers for the whole moon fiasco. He would do what he could to keep Raven safe in the press, as he always did.

"Office."

"I figured."

"See you soon," Scott said, emphasizing the soon. If Raven were living full time in NeoLondon again, he had no excuse for not meeting his friend every once in a while. Maybe returning to the resistance was a good idea after all.

"Thanks, Scott," Raven said, and hugged him tightly. "Give my love to Lydia and tell her I'll see her soon too."

As Raven stood up, a few more people in the bookstore noticed him and left. Scott paid little attention; he needed to get a ride and taxis rarely came to the lower levels. He kept switching between happiness and fear for Raven, and he couldn't decide if Raven's move was a good, sound decision or another hastily made mistake. Raven seemed happy, though, and that was what mattered most. He knew Raven would never have an ordinary life; Scott just wanted him to have a life surrounded by people who loved him.

AFTER RAVEN and the other man split up, Atheus followed the former. He had been waiting for days for someone to report on Raven's presence and he had started to wonder if Raven had left the city for good. Atheus had people searching on all levels of the city but most of his effort was on the lower levels, where Raven might feel more protected. It had worked, and now Atheus would finally be able to track him back and find the resistance's headquarters.

Atheus was in human form, not díamont form, so Raven wouldn't recognize him. He hardly recognized himself sometimes. His human body was aging faster than he liked and it was only a matter of time before it gave out entirely. Maybe fifty, sixty more years. The scientists who had built Atheus added aging as a safety mechanism so that he couldn't live forever. Medane was aging as well, though it didn't seem to be as fast, Atheus thought jealously. Medane still had all of his hair, and his darker skin hid some of the wrinkles. Only Lethe was created to live forever. And if there was a way to make Lethe live forever, there had to be a way to duplicate it and allow himself to live forever as well. Death was for humans, not for díamonts.

Raven was hard to follow through the city but Atheus already had a general idea where he would end up. Kaela had refused to give the specific location of the rebel's headquarters, the bitch, but he would deal with her later. Atheus glared at the thought of her and a passerby flinched and hurried past. He controlled his face. In díamont form his emotions were always hidden and he often forgot to appear calm in human form. Raven had told the other man he was staying with Nalia, the girl. The díamont, Atheus corrected himself. As soon as Medane mentioned the rogue díamont, Atheus had known where it came from and eliminated everyone with connections to the lab. Lethe wouldn't be able to find a trace.

And she wore the bracelet, Atheus thought with malicious glee. It was designed for Medane, of course. With Medane out of the way, Lethe would be relatively easy to manipulate and Atheus would finally be free to research immortality. The bracelet was like a bomb, in many ways, but it depended on díamont DNA to function. If Medane touched it, he would be killed almost instantly and the blast would take out a huge area as well. On the girl, though, it seemed to be taking longer. The little brat had even managed to channel the explosive power somehow when she attacked him, using it like a laser gun. Not for long, though, he knew. It would slowly eat away at her body, sapping her strength and wreaking havoc on a microscopic level until it consumed her entirely.

And Raven was with her now, Atheus thought. This pleased him; Raven had escaped Atheus as a child but surely the fool would be willing to serve Atheus if it meant saving that girl's life. Atheus was even willing to throw in Kaela's life as well. If Raven did what Atheus wanted, he was prepared to let all three live out their lives according to his plan.

Raven entered a building with a shabby exterior and open door. Atheus remained hidden, knowing that his dark clothing would attract attention from the peasants here. Luckily they weren't smart enough to post guards or they would have seen him. Atheus made a note of the location and waited long enough to make sure that Raven didn't go anywhere else. Then Atheus headed back to the main city and started making calls. There were plenty of people who would enjoy taking Raven down and they would surely be interested in knowing where he was. Atheus was prepared to pay top dollar for Raven, as long as he was alive. Atheus was also prepared to kill anyone who murdered Raven before Atheus had the chance. His contacts would know not to cross him, Atheus knew. It was only a matter of time now before Raven was his.

CHAPTER 8

Nalia found herself gardening once again, but for the first time, it didn't even occur to her to complain. Raven was with her, pulling out weeds at her side, both of them laughing when the dirt flew and the roots snapped. She had never imagined that physical labor could be fun. Her father didn't approve, she knew, but she didn't care. She didn't believe the things he said about Raven either. Maybe Raven used to be selfish and callous, but he didn't seem like it anymore.

She pulled out a carrot carefully and brushed off the dust. There was a lump on the vegetable, hard and almost shell-like. She showed it to Raven and his eyes widened. He grabbed the lump and lifted it off the carrot, flipping it over to show her the other side of the shell. It was slimy, and it moved in place. She fought the urge to drop the carrot and run from the garden. She hated bugs and never expected to find one outside like this.

"It's a snail," Raven said.

He didn't sound frightened. She tried to match his tone.

"What's that?"

"A wild animal. They used to live everywhere, but now they're just in the far north and south. I don't know what it's doing in the middle of the city."

Nalia looked at the thing with honest curiosity. Like every other child, she had seen pets before, and zoo animals, and museum animals, and like every city-dweller, she dealt with insects on a regular basis. It looked too small to be an animal, but it clearly wasn't a bug. She reached out and he handed it to her. She gingerly held it by the hard case, watching the flat part on the bottom squirm. The case didn't move. Maybe it was a shell like some bugs had. Raven took it from her again and set it back on the carrot, lifting the carrot between them horizontally. After a moment, the flat part started shifting and two stalks rose from the front. Nalia could just make out something like eyes on the ends.

"Wow," she said, not knowing what else to say. "Should we bring it somewhere? Outside the city or something where it can live?"

"It seems to be happy here," Raven said, glancing at the nearby produce. "There must be more of them somewhere nearby. We'll have to be more careful when we're out here."

She nodded. The word 'we' sounded especially good. They finished collecting the ripe vegetables and returned inside. Klaus was at the stove, as usual, and Raven quickly excused himself and went upstairs. Klaus had grudgingly lent him the use of one of the spare rooms. Nalia set the basket down and told him about the animal.

"Well, the soil is from a rural area," Klaus said, sounding disinterested.

She wondered if he really felt that way or if he were just being difficult because Raven had been interested in the animal. Nalia couldn't figure out a way to make Klaus see that Raven had changed and that Raven sincerely regretted the loss of lives at the Graveyard Massacre. They hadn't talked about it, exactly, but she could tell. Raven looked around sometimes like he was seeing ghosts and his behavior around Klaus and other relatives of the deceased was much more withdrawn than he was with Nalia.

"Last week's march in Paris went well, I heard," Nalia said. "You talked to the rep?"

The European representative was a thin man who visited every week with news. Normally he insisted on talking to Nalia and Nalia alone, but she had been gone when he arrived. Klaus said the rep had wanted to stage a full search and immediately blame the government for interference. Personally, Nalia thought the rep just wanted a few minutes alone with her. The thought disgusted her; his flirting was so crude and over-the-top. But Klaus said he was important to the movement so Nalia put up with him. She even led him on, a little, just for fun. It was kind of nice knowing that someone thought she was beautiful, even if she thought he was slimier than the snail had been.

"He said everything was peaceful, they made their point and the police allowed the march. Doesn't think it's going to change anything. The European state is the weakest in the Eastern World. We need protests in all major cities in all the states before something happens."

Nalia agreed. She didn't bring up the fact that he was almost quoting something Raven had said earlier about the movement's realistic chances of being heard. Raven had been quite pessimistic about the matter but he had offered good, sound advice that even Klaus found appealing.

"I've been trying," Nalia said. "But the weather's so bad right now for so many places, it's hard. We might have to wait for winter, or at least fall."

It was an argument she had heard before, and one she had given. Marching in NeoLondon or Paris was one thing, but expecting the same in NeoCairo or Seoul was entirely different. Below the 40th parallel, going outside in the summer was rarely even an option. Most places had either violent desert storms or heavy humidity and monsoons, and people remained in the carefully fortified cities as much as possible. While Nalia did expect her people to be willing to risk their lives for liberty and equal rights, she didn't want anyone hurt unnecessarily. Winters weren't much better, but a larger number of people were able to move freely then.

"I was thinking of asking Raven to contact the African states to see—"

Klaus sighed heavily and Nalia stopped in annoyance.

"Look, father, he's helping us now and we might as well make use of his connections."

"He's helping us now," Klaus conceded. "But why? He has an ulterior motive, I'm sure. And even if he doesn't, he's just going to leave eventually. You shouldn't count on him for long-term support. Or anything, for that matter."

Nalia resumed putting away the vegetables. It was impossible to talk to her father about anything relating to Raven. She shouldn't have even tried, but the thought of all the possibilities his presence opened up was exciting to her. She wanted to share that excitement with someone.

"Look, Nalia," Klaus said, stopping his work and taking her hand. He led her to the table and sat down, keeping her hands in his. "I know you think I'm being harsh with him. I know Bryce is a good person at heart. He was then, he is now. And I know that he takes his responsibilities very seriously, and I'm sure your mother's death was as traumatic for him as it was for all of us. But you have to understand that he's done things since then, terrible things. He's killed people, Nalia, you know that."

Nalia lowered her head. She did know. Raven never tried to deny it. He didn't talk about his past much, not directly. It was just hard to imagine a sane, intelligent person taking another person's life on purpose. Raven was sane, he was intelligent, and Nalia simply couldn't believe that it was true. Maybe he had caused people's deaths, or been in some way responsible. But it shouldn't be possible for one human to deliberately take the life of another. That was what Kaonism taught, and what Nalia believed. People died to protect what they loved, people sometimes killed to protect as well, but those people were never the same after.

It was why murder or any form of killing resulted in the death penalty in the Western World. One of the images that Nalia and the others used to protest Kaonite laws was the picture of a young woman, a new mother. She had been driving her child to the doctor when a man jumped from an over passing walkway and landed on her car. She crashed and the man died, with a suicide note strapped to his chest. She and her child were injured but alive. She was given a trial and sentenced to death because she had been driving the car that caused the man's death. Motive didn't matter in Kaonite courts, but it did matter to Nalia. Maybe Raven had been forced into similar situations where he had killed someone on accident, or because there were no other options.

"Well," Klaus said, awkwardly removing his hands and rubbing them on his apron as he stood up, "I just want you to know that I do understand. I do. But he isn't who he appears to be, and I don't want you to get hurt."

"Thanks, Daddy," she said.

He looked pleased by the name; she hadn't called him Daddy since her first transformation into a díamont. Since then, he had been more of a coach and instructor than a real father. Nalia hadn't even considered that he might have her best interests in mind. She had assumed he was trapped in the past, stuck on his wife's death, but he was only trying to look out for her. She offered to help in the kitchen and he accepted, and Nalia couldn't remember the last time they had felt so peaceful together.

RAVEN HAD BEEN LIVING in the slums for several days now and hadn't slept soundly a single night. It wasn't just the memories of his time here, he thought as he pulled the thin blanket to his chin and attempted to relax. It was seeing Nalia and her father interact. He could remember a time in his life when he had parents who cared for him the way Klaus cared for Nalia. Every time he fell asleep, he had the same dream. The dream was based in memory, he knew, and it had haunted him his entire life. The dream had changed over time but not much. It always started with his mother singing a lullaby, and images and words and sounds from the dream leaked into his mind whenever he shut his eyes.

I am six when they are killed. Too old to be sung to sleep, but my father is working late and my mother is giving me extra attention. Her voice is sweet and gentle, and I know that I am loved. Completely, unconditionally loved. I am safe. My mother is at my side; my father will be home soon to kiss my forehead goodnight.

Even in the dream Raven luxuriated in the feeling of safety, wishing the dream would end before the feeling was shattered. But the dream always shifted to another scene.

I am asleep, thumb in my mouth, feet dangling out of the covers. A loud burst of sound like a tree snapping in freezing rain. I open my eyes and look around. There is talking in the hall, my mother's voice only it is pleading and desperate like I've never heard. Another burst and her voice stops. Other people talk. Strangers. They are looking for other people in my home. They go downstairs and I run to my parents' room.

My mother is on the floor. Her body is there in a white and gold paisley nightgown that I helped my father pick out for her birthday last year. It has red streaks on it. My father is on the bed. I hear gasping, suckling sounds and his chest goes up and down. The sounds stop and I wait for him to stand up and hold me close to his chest and wrap his arms all the way around me. His arms are so long I sometimes think he could wrap me up twice if he tried. But he doesn't get up.

I am angry, in a way I have never been before. I hear footsteps approaching and a voice calling my name. "Where are you, Bryce?" I don't care how he knows my name. I have a gun in my hand now and I want nothing more than to do to this man what he did to my parents. I walk into the hallway and confront him. I am smiling and hating him as I pull the trigger and it is ecstasy because I have won.

Raven knew the dream wasn't entirely true. Over the years, the ending had shifted. Raven suspected it was because of his job working for the government. He *had* killed the intruder, he knew, but he didn't remember the details, like how he had gotten a gun. He thought that his parents might have kept one for protection. It wasn't illegal at that time. And he had been a child, far too young for the pure hatred and pleasure he felt at the end of the dream.

But the dream that had haunted him his entire life terrified him for more reasons than just the emotional trauma. It marked him as a killer. He had been a killer at the age of six, and because he lived in Portland, because the police found him with a gun in his hands, he was sentenced to death. Only the actions of a kind police officer who smuggled him to the Eastern World had saved his life. Raven had never been back to the Western World because he knew that if he did, he could be brought up on charges of murder and killed. He had confessed to the crime, after all, and even though it seemed insane that a court system would accept the confession of a child only hours after he witnessed his parents' deaths, it was damning evidence against him. When he began working for Medane, Raven was always careful to leave no trace of his presence. People suspected he was involved, but there was no evidence linking him to any murders in the Eastern World. Just the West.

In the middle of the night, alone in the dark like this, Raven could admit that the most frightening part of the dream was the feeling of pleasure when he pulled the trigger. Every single time Raven was sent on a mission to kill, he knew that there was a chance that this feeling would envelop him in real life. He only accepted jobs where he would have a chance to eliminate a criminal or murderer. Usually they had been sanctioned by the government, but overstepped their limits. He had killed six people in the Lower African state once, all militia members, because they had slaughtered two rural villages and covered it up by claiming a plague had hit. Raven hadn't meant to kill any of them, but he was visiting the state and overheard their plans for another 'plague' to strike. The joy in their voices when they thought of killing helpless humans was too much.

He killed because he hated to kill, because he regretted it and honored the people he killed. It was the only thing that separated him from the people he despised and every time he took a life, he begged fate not to turn him into his nightmare. Every time was terrifying. He had killed twenty-seven men and women in his life, including his parents' killer. Not including the people who had died as a result of his decisions. That number was far greater.

Raven wondered whether the world would be better off without him. He tried so hard to help people and protect them. He wanted to be a hero. But no matter what he did, it seemed like the people he loved were the ones hurt. Nalia's mother was killed because of what he believed. Kaela's life was at risk because he decided to destroy the moon records. Even Scott, his dearest friend in the world, had been forced to give up so many opportunities in order to help Raven.

A soft knock at the door brought Raven instantly to his feet. He had hardwired his door with a code to prevent intruders, but intruders wouldn't knock. Raven adjusted his loose pants and opened the door, expecting to see Klaus or another member of the resistance. It was Nalia.

"Can I come in?"

He gestured and she walked in, leaving him bewildered at the door. Habit led him to close the door and reset the code, but he didn't know what to do next. Nalia was in a thin tank top and shorts, both vivid pink. Her skin looked pale and shadowed in comparison, though nothing could really diminish her beauty. She circled his room before sitting on the edge of the bed.

"I couldn't sleep," she said.

He took a few steps closer but didn't sit next to her. She was gorgeous. The moon was shining through the small window; the only light in the room. She tucked her knees up and wrapped her arms around them, cocking her head at him.

"Sit down?"

He sat near her, but far enough away that they weren't touching. His heart was beating loudly and he couldn't stop thinking about the dream, and his fears. How would he end up hurting Nalia? She was so precious to him, like a star that hadn't fallen from the sky yet, a single flake of snow before it landed and dissolved into a billion flakes just like it. In Nalia, he saw everything he wanted to be, everything he could have been if he had just been more careful and less selfish. He wanted nothing more than to protect her.

"How are you?" she asked, stretching a hand out to take his.

He started at the touch. Her hand was surprisingly cool for the hot weather and soft against his bare skin. He suddenly realized that he was only wearing an undershirt, not the full-sleeved shirts he was used to having people see him in. She didn't seem to mind, though.

"You're being awfully quiet. Is everything okay?"

He blinked and felt his cheeks warm. She sounded worried. About him. It was strange having someone show so much tenderness toward him. She moved her hand up to his arm, to his shoulder, and across his back, leaning her body until it rested against his, her head tucked under his. The way he used to tuck his head under his mother's, he thought with a shudder.

"Sorry," he said when she straightened.

She must have thought he was shuddering at her. He wrapped his arms around her and wondered if this was what his parents felt when they held him. He wanted to protect her so much. Nothing could be allowed to happen to her.

Raven's computer flashed red from where it sat on the floor near the door. He removed himself from Nalia to check. His heart skipped. Intruders, real intruders, hacking through the code on his door. It looked like they would be successful, too. They must have been waiting for night to get to him. Unless they were after Nalia, he thought in panic. No. That would not happen.

"Nalia, people are about to break in," he whispered. "You are going to hide. Here."

He pulled open a hatch under the bed. Like almost all of the rooms in this building, it had a secret door into the hidden corridors that led down to the underground bunker. The first thing he had done upon entering this room was locate that entrance in case of emergency. Nalia didn't look surprised by the hatch, so she obviously knew about the building's history, but she did look angry.

"I'm not hiding," she said. "If people are breaking in, I'll fight them."

"No," Raven said fiercely. "You don't want to fight these people. They'll kill you, or you'll kill them."

Raven trembled at the thought of Nalia having to kill someone. He only barely managed to recover from each kill he made. She didn't have the experience or maturity to deal with death the way he had learned. She crossed her arms and didn't move. He changed tactics. The door would only hold for a minute or two. She had to be safe.

"Take my computer, go in the hatch and wait. No matter what you hear, wait for ten minutes. Ten. No matter what. Then you can come out and help me if I need help. But not until then. Please. Please," he repeated.

She climbed under the bed, computer in hand, and down the hatch. He slid it shut and grabbed his gun. The door opened and dark figures entered. He couldn't tell how many.

He fired once, hit someone. Someone else fired back, two people fired back, Raven returned the shots blindly and something struck his ankle. Not a bullet. A person pummeled toward him and knocked the gun from his hand. He fought. He saw a syringe on the floor at the same time his ankle and foot started going numb. Another person punched him and he punched back. There was blood on his fist from the other person's face. The room started spinning and Raven was lying on the ground, trying to kick the person standing over him and failing. White streamers trailed across his vision, blocking the faces of the people who leaned to look at him. Strong hands grabbed his arms and feet and he felt himself carried somewhere. He wondered if Nalia was safe. He hoped she waited. He blacked out.

CHAPTER 9

Medane stared at Lethe's impassive face on the screen as Lethe informed him that Atheus had already returned to the Western World with Kaela. She would be safe, Medane hoped. Kaela was too valuable to risk. Atheus planned on using her to continue the breeding project, so her health and her ability to reproduce would be protected. Psychologically, however, Atheus would probably be merciless. The project was intended to create humans who were intelligent, fast, and strong, and in Kaela and Raven's generation it had finally succeeded. One of the scientists hired by Atheus believed that those traits could be put into overdrive by stressing the individual. Raven had been the first target; Atheus had ordered the boy's parents murdered in order to observe his reaction. Raven responded just as the scientist had predicted: in the minutes after the boy realized his parents were dead, he had moved faster than the eye could follow, chased the murderer, and killed him. By the time Medane and the police arrived, Raven was in a state of shock and could barely move at all.

Lethe sat stiffly on the other end of the screen, hands flat on the desk. His face was calm as always, but Medane knew he was angry.

"Given the recent disappearance of your agent, Raven," Lethe said, "Atheus believes that the United Western World government needs his assistance and I gave him permission to leave. I know that this will make it more difficult to locate the rogue díamont, but I cannot put his nation at risk."

"You don't really think the Eastern World would attack, do you?"

"I don't know what to think," Lethe said. His voice was faster than usual and he sounded frustrated. "But the moon will be in communication again in a matter of days and if you were responsible for whatever happened, it would make sense for you to want Atheus trapped in the East where he can't order a retaliation."

"I told you," Medane said. "Raven acted alone on the moon base and Atheus has agreed not to pursue charges."

"Raven has also vanished. It has been suggested that he is assisting the rogue díamont."

"Atheus suggested that, I suppose?"

Lethe didn't respond.

Medane shook his head in frustration. Raven was his main concern. The boy's rash move had put him at extreme risk and all Medane could do was prevent the Eastern World from naming him an enemy of the state. It had taken a long conference with the Eastern President to convince her that Raven wasn't a threat. As long as Raven stayed near NeoLondon and as long as Atheus didn't return to the West, Raven would be relatively safe.

But once Atheus returned to his own government and resumed his position of power, he would regain access to the West's nuclear arsenal. Medane didn't believe that Atheus would use the weapons; he and Atheus had both been in the nuclear blast that destroyed old London and crippled Soren. Even if they weren't used, though, they were a threat. The United Western World could declare Raven a terrorist for his attack on the moon base and retaliate against anyone shielding him—including the United Eastern World government.

"If he is helping the rogue díamont, then he is not doing it on my orders."

"Unless you can prove that, I have to allow Atheus to return to the West. I will not leave the West unprotected."

Oh, Raven, Medane thought. He knew Raven was helping the díamont, or at least the same resistance movement that the díamont supported. It was a cause that Raven felt deeply about. Medane had seen Raven enter the same overdrive state that had driven him to his first kill when Raven led nearly sixty of his followers into a rooftop graveyard in order to break into the government building. They succeeded and Medane had been forced to protect the President from enemy fire before the police responded and drove them back out to the graveyard. The rebels were trapped and disorganized, and the police had killed most of them when Raven—moving faster than the bullets fired at him—rescued the survivors and pulled them to safety. Again, Medane believed the stress of watching his loved ones die pushed him into superhuman speed.

"I've made my decision," Lethe said firmly. "Atheus is returning to the West and bringing Kaela with him. You will continue looking for the rogue díamont and you will contact me immediately when you find him."

Medane agreed and shut the screen. Kaela would be moderately safe, but Raven was in great danger with Atheus gone. Medane knew that Kaela had been put under the same stress as Raven, although he didn't know the specifics. He knew her parents were killed when she was young, but she hadn't been present and hadn't reacted the same way Raven had. But something must have pushed her into Atheus' employment. Atheus must have pressured her into committing some crime and then blackmailed her afterward. Medane hated thinking of his old friend in that light, but it made sense. And now that Atheus had Kaela again, there was no chance of giving the girl a chance at a real life.

He knew Raven hadn't meant to cause so much chaos when he disrupted communication with the moon base. Raven probably just saw an opportunity to enforce the law banning díamont research. He might have gotten away without the West finding out about his involvement if he hadn't kidnapped Kaela as well. Medane had barely smoothed that over when Raven quit, leaving Medane and the entire Eastern World at the mercy of both Atheus and the rogue díamont. Atheus would take personal revenge if he could. He had already set a price on Raven's head. Medane was just glad the bounty required Raven to be alive.

Nalia flinched at the sound of the first gunshot. She pressed her hand against the latch over her head at the explosion of gunfire that followed. She knew Raven wanted to keep her safe, but did he really expect her to just crouch here in the darkness between the floors while he was killed? She was not going to wait ten minutes. She would wait until the fighting slowed or stopped. She could hear muffled sounds of people moving and talking. The bottom of the wooden latch scratched against her palm. She had known about this passageway, of course, but she had never been in it. The walls were plaster and didn't offer much protection if a bullet pierced through. She knew he had wanted her to move to safety but she remained directly underneath his room and waited.

As soon as there was silence, she gripped the latch and shoved upwards. It hit against the bed frame with a crash. She braced herself for an attack, but the room seemed empty. She pushed the latch up slowly and wedged herself through, climbing from under the bed into a pool of luke-warm water. It was dark, only the moonlight shining through. No one was there.

The door slammed open and Nalia lifted her fists the way her father had taught her. A light switched on and she was temporarily blinded. She blinked rapidly until the light stopped stinging, and looked around. Klaus and three hefty members of the resistance stood at the doorway with mouths open. The floor was covered in maroon streaks and puddles. Not water. Blood. The trail continued out the door. Klaus signaled for the others to follow the trail and they vanished down the hall. Nalia couldn't move.

Her hands were covered in blood. Not water. She had crawled through blood to get up. Wet, thick, crimson liquid drying on her skin. Her hands started rubbing her shorts as if they had a mind of their own, desperate to be clean. Red stained her pink shorts and her eyes blurred with tears.

"Honey," her father said.

He took her hands in his and stopped their frantic movement.

"Are you hurt?" he asked.

She shook her head, then shivered. Her whole body felt defiled by the violence around her. And the blood. Klaus led her into the bathroom and started running the shower. She took a step forward to get into it but her father stopped her and motioned her to undress, politely turning his back. She pulled her clothes off and stepped into the water. Hot. It was burning. She shut her eyes against the pain and said nothing. She needed to be burned. Her skin was probably turning red from the heat, red like the blood on her hands. Her father suggested turning the water colder but she ignored him. Eyes closed, she let the steam and water cleanse her.

Nalia had never seen something like that before. She wondered what had happened, if Raven was safe. Or if Raven had killed someone. She shivered and leaned into the water, letting it burn across her closed eyes. She knew he had killed someone. The shapes of the blurs on the floor. People must have attacked him, he fired, they fought back, and he killed someone and dragged the body outside. She wondered if he thought that by disposing of the body, it changed the fact that he had killed another human. He was a killer. She had been so close to him, touching him, enjoying him, thinking that he was a real person like her. But he wasn't. Klaus was right. There was no way Raven could be a normal person after the things that he had done.

When the water started to run cold, a warm towel was handed to her. Klaus helped her step out of the shower. The air was thick with steam but she could still feel the blood on her hands, and the feel of Raven's skin. Klaus held out a nightgown for her. He hadn't helped her dress since before she went to Seoul, long before her mother had died. She liked having his attention. She knew that *he* would never kill anyone.

Nalia finally opened her eyes to see her father's face red and blotchy from the heat and tears. He hugged her like she was a child again.

"Where is he," she whispered, not really wanting to know. She never wanted to see Raven again.

"Gone," Klaus said.

"Good."

She closed her eyes and held her father close. She was taller than him, she realized with surprise. Not much, not enough to notice when they faced each, but obvious when they were so close. She snuggled her head into his neck. She didn't want to be taller. She wanted to be his little girl again.

"He was the target," Klaus said. It sounded like the words were strangling him but he kept going. "We found a drugged dart. They must have overpowered him and drugged him, then kidnapped him. Atheus placed a reward on him, alive. We just found out."

Nalia looked at her father. "He didn't kill anyone?"

"I don't know," Klaus admitted. "I heard five gunshots and we only found three bullets in the room. But if he did," Klaus' face grew cloudy and he squeezed her shoulders. "It was self-defense, Nalia."

"Not if they didn't plan on killing him," Nalia said.

She was furious that her father seemed to be siding with Raven. She had finally realized that Klaus was right about Raven being a killer; Klaus had no right to change his mind now.

"He didn't know that."

Nalia's lip jutted forward and she knew she looked like a pouting child, but she couldn't help it. She was confused and couldn't figure out what she was supposed to be feeling. Anger. Definitely. But towards whom? Raven, for killing someone? Or for treating her like a child and making her hide? Her father seemed like he was trying to help her but his words were just upsetting her more. She was mostly angry at whoever had broken in, she decided. Hired assassins, probably, if they were responding to a bounty. People who valued money over life. Scum.

"Where did they take him?" she finally asked.

She didn't know how she felt but she knew it was her responsibility to take care of Raven if he was in trouble. She had hired him, after all.

"We don't know. A few people saw a car drive off but no one knew enough to follow."

They couldn't go to the police for help tracking the car, Nalia knew. Not since Raven had left Medane's service. The police might have even been the ones to take him. Nalia let out a sigh. Her first priority was finding Raven and making sure he was alive. That was more important than anything else, she told herself. Even more important than knowing whether or not he had killed someone just a few feet away from her, just moments after they had held each so closely. No. She would ignore that for now. First, she needed to find him.

CHAPTER 10

The monitor on Atheus' left blinked. Medane was attempting to contact him. Atheus and Kaela were nearly back in the United Western World, safely ensconced in Atheus' private plane. Lethe had agreed to give Atheus a few hours before informing Medane. Atheus loved how easily he could manipulate Lethe into thinking of Medane as the enemy. Medane had practically set himself up, and Atheus was already trying to figure out how to lay all the blame from the new díamont on Medane's head.

Atheus shut the monitor off. Technically, it was illegal to use visual communication during flight. Medane had implemented that rule. Even though monitors were built into every plane model, they weren't used for communication because Medane was worried about an increase in crashes. Atheus didn't bother with the details; it was usually better to humor Medane, and it kept Medane under the impression that Atheus cared about the humans. The longer Medane believed that, the longer Atheus had to find a way to kill him.

Atheus felt a shallow sympathy for his friend. He remembered the Last War and how close he had been to Medane. They had shared everything. Hopes, dreams, fears... Mostly fears, as the war continued. They felt betrayed by their brother Soren and horrified by his actions and the deaths he was causing, but neither of them ever asked Soren why he was doing it until just before his death. Not his death, Atheus corrected himself. The nuclear blast that disabled all three of them. It was essentially Soren's death, however, since he never woke up. When Medane left to get the bomb, Atheus had tried his hardest to keep Soren in one place. He didn't want the díamont causing any more damage and he knew he had to delay Soren until Medane could return. Atheus had succeeded, in a way, but Soren had spoken to him. Soren, silver-tongued snake that he was, always managed to persuade people to agree with him and Atheus was on guard. But Soren had made no attempt to plead for his life or even use his friendship with Atheus to save himself. Instead, he had leaned close to Atheus.

"We are gods, Atheus," Soren had whispered. "We will never be merely human. We can be immortal—"

Medane had thrown the bomb just then and the world exploded into darkness. When Atheus and Medane regained consciousness and learned that the humans had finally discovered a way to kill díamonts, Soren's words echoed in his mind. Immortal. Atheus was kind to Lethe, of course. They all wanted to rid the world of Soren. And Lethe had returned the kindness by refusing to kill Atheus and Medane and choosing instead to let them live in peace. Once Atheus realized that he would survive the Last War, Soren's words became stronger and more appealing. The díamonts *were* gods, after all. The humans had created them to be exactly that: nonhumans with incredible powers. How dare the humans presume to destroy the gods they had created?

Atheus glanced at the clock next to the monitor. They would be landing in less than an hour. Medane would be furious. Atheus couldn't keep back a smile at the thought of his friend pacing in his NeoLondon office, helpless to prevent his precious Raven from being returned to the Western World. About time, too. Kaela was in prime childbearing years and the superhuman genome must continue. So far Kaela had refused the men Atheus deemed appropriate. Atheus would not allow over a century of work isolating and strengthening the human genome to be thrown aside, certainly not because his subjects were unwilling to reproduce.

Kaela's children, and Raven's, if he had any, would be useful, but the combination of the two made Atheus shiver. It would be a perfect human, capable of the superhuman feats of both its parents, human enough to rule the world openly. Under Atheus' control, of course. As a díamont, he was prevented from an open position of power. The díamonts were weapons, not politicians, and they were universally feared after the Last War. But a child produced by Kaela and Raven would be accepted, and once Atheus had both of them under his control, raising the child would be no problem.

Except for Medane, Atheus thought angrily. Medane would interfere the way he had with Raven. Under Medane's control, Raven had become headstrong and independent, capable of thinking for himself and choosing his own future. Unacceptable. Atheus had done a far better job with Kaela. He glanced at the woman seated across from him. Kaela was pale and hadn't spoken a word. She knew she was in trouble and she was probably just hoping to escape with her life. Exactly the type of obedience Atheus wanted. She would have no thoughts of running away, he knew. She would try to prove her loyalty in an attempt to save herself, and in doing so, she would become an even more valuable servant.

RAVEN'S HEAD pounded against his ears, pulsing white starry pain in his eyes as the sound blocked out all other perceptions. Bitter vinegar filled his mouth and nose and he couldn't feel his body. Raven tried to calm his racing thoughts. He could sense people around him, vague shapes of heat and whispering. Something cold landed on his lips and they opened instinctively. He felt his body swallow liquid and wondered if it were poison.

His brain felt as though it were swelling up and about to explode and his ears were about to burst. So much pressure, but it was hurting less. The throbbing headache was almost reassuring; the only part of his body he could feel and control. Raven tried to open his eyes. It took several tries before he remembered how to lift the eyelids, and long minutes before he recognized outlines in the blur before his eyes and could make sense of his vision.

He was lying down in a vehicle. There was a man sitting across from him. The man had a thick purple scar where his eye must have once been. He looked familiar but Raven couldn't place him. The man noticed Raven looking around and his scarred face twisted into something that could have been a grimace or a grin.

"Good morning," the man said. His voice was familiar, too, but Raven couldn't keep his mind focused long enough to remember. It hurt too much to think.

Another voice came from above his head, maybe the front of the vehicle. It felt like an airship—there was some turbulence but nothing like cars. And the constant pressure in his head could be due to high elevation, Raven thought.

"We don't want him awake yet," the second, female voice said.

It also sounded familiar.

"He can't do anything."

"I don't want to take chances."

The man across from Raven laughed. He leaned forward until his face was inches from Raven's, leering down at him. Lower Africa, Raven remembered. Botswana. The man was one of the black-clothed elite allowed to kill, but he had slipped poison into a river providing drinking water for thousands. Medane had forbidden Raven from killing the man —he had too many powerful allies—but Raven had taken his eye in return for the innocent lives this man had needlessly taken. Raven couldn't move, trapped on his back with no sense of his body. He couldn't fight or protect himself. He could only hope the pain that enveloped his mind with each heartbeat would eventually leave and he would be able to move again.

The man pressed a hand on Raven's cheek. He barely felt it and wondered what drug they had given him. The man's thumb lowered over Raven's right eye, closing the lid. Raven couldn't feel if he were pressing or not. He couldn't feel anything except the pressure in his head.

"He's safe enough," the man said smugly, taking his hand away.

Raven wondered what the man had done. Surely he would feel pain if the man had damaged his eye, Raven thought. But he couldn't see out of it, and couldn't remember how to open it again. His open eye watered, not with pain but with frustration at his complete helplessness. The man moved back across the vehicle and ignored him.

Time passed. Minutes. Hours. Raven couldn't tell. He managed to shut both eyes, and open them. His right eye was fine. The man occasionally reached out to hit his arm. Lightly, just testing if Raven could feel it. Raven was careful to remain motionless even after sensation returned in his arms, his legs, his torso. His head was still on the verge of exploding but the pain seemed to be getting less as his body regained its strength. He didn't move, kept his eyes and face blank, and waited until he could get the upper hand.

They were definitely on a plane, Raven decided as the vehicle dipped downward. They would be landing soon and that was when he needed to move. The scarred man seemed to be taking some pleasure in seeing Raven helpless like this, so perhaps he would continue ignoring his partner's advice and leave Raven unbound. He wondered who the woman was. Her voice was familiar, but he knew she wasn't from either African state.

"Is he awake?" she called from the front.

"He can't do anything," the man reassured her, punching Raven hard.

It took all of Raven's discipline to allow the man to punch him. He needed the man to think he was still helpless, otherwise he wouldn't be able to escape. The pressure in his head was easing as they continued the descent and Raven did his best to remain limp when they touched down. He still had no idea where they were or what kind of plane this was, but it seemed like a small plane and the runway was bumpy as they slowed, so it probably wasn't a major airport.

The plane stopped and the man stood up, checking Raven with another punch. A woman appeared near Raven's head; the pilot. She wore khaki slacks and a black vest and Raven didn't need to hear her speak again to recognize her. One of the assassins from the Chinese state. She used to be sanctioned by the government until Raven had exposed a plot of hers to eliminate a group of monks living in the mountains. The monks had peacefully declined to be in the Chinese state, preferring instead to remain outside the world governments' control. Normally Raven would have approved of forcing resisters to join the government, but the monks were an exception. They were pacifists and only had limited communication with the outside world. When this woman had tried to kill them, Raven had stepped in and she was exiled. He hadn't seen or heard of her again, until now.

The man and woman conferred in low voices before popping open the door. Heat poured in. Wherever they were was much farther south than NeoLondon. Raven tried to learn as much as he could without moving. Dry air, no humidity. Desert area. Probably one of the African states, maybe the Chinese state. The woman leapt out of the door, probably to get steps or a ramp. Most planes were a good height from the ground and there was no way they could carry an unconscious body—which they thought he was—without some sort of assistance.

Raven considered his options. The woman would be gone for a few seconds. Raven could attack the man, jump from the plane, and hope they were in a public airport with access to the outside. Or he could continue biding his time and wait to see if they were in a military enclosure. There was no point giving up the element of surprise if it turned out the plane was completely surrounded by enemies. He wanted to attack now, his fingers trembled with the urge, but he fought it. He needed more information before he acted.

Steps appeared out the door and the woman climbed up and secured the plane. The man grabbed Raven roughly and tossed him over his shoulder. Raven let his arms and legs hang limp. His face was pressed against the man's rough ebony shirt and it smelled of sweat and sour vinegar. Traces of the poison they used, Raven thought. The smell had an affect; he felt dizzy again and it wasn't hard to pretend that he had no control over his body. He was jostled down the metal staircase and tried to look around.

Heat waves wafted from the black asphalt and made vision difficult. Outside. Raven tried to avoid breathing in the sickening poison fumes and wondered how the man wasn't affected. Some people around, but not too many. He caught a glimpse of a military uniform and unconsciously flinched. It bore the seal of the United Western World.

"Don't wake up yet," the man said, reaching around to slap his head.

The pain was extreme and for a few moments Raven could barely breathe for fear of vomiting. The West. He couldn't be in the West. The man grabbed his waist and dropped Raven to the ground. He was dizzy and sick with fear and pain. His captors were focused on three approaching figures so he didn't have to worry about being seen as he squinted to see who was coming. His heart shuddered as he saw the sunlight reflecting crimson off the central figure. Atheus.

Raven barely had time to collect his strength before he was on his feet. The man and woman had no time to react: Raven crippled them with blows to the face and groin. Nonfatal. But painful. Atheus shouted something and Raven ran. No fence enclosed the airport and Raven sprinted. Each step jarred against his temples. His legs trembled but he urged them to keep running, keep going until he found something. People were following him on foot but they were no match. Raven had always been fast and he had a reason to run now. He was in the Western World, and so was Atheus. Raven would be killed.

CHAPTER 11

Scott introduced Lydia to his fellow writers, his editors, the copy staff, the technicians, everyone, in fact, who happened to be in the United Eastern Press building. He couldn't contain his wide grin and loved the compliments and congratulations from his peers. This was the first time any of them had met Lydia in person before and Scott preened as he presented his beautiful wife. She looked especially beautiful today, he thought. She was dressed in white, the traditional color for the moon, with silver earrings and bracelets. Even her shoes were silver sandals. She looked like the stereotypical moon girl from advertisements, only far more gorgeous.

Scott's colleagues were duly impressed, maybe even jealous, Scott thought happily. He endured a fair share of teasing since his wife lived so far away. A few of his colleagues even suspected that the 'wife' was an invention and Scott really had secret lover in the government. The rumor had probably started when he and Raven had been living together, and some of Scott's co-workers found it suspicious that he always knew where to get the latest scoop on government stories. They knew he had some connection with an insider and romance was far more interesting and easy to understand than the deep-rooted, unreserved love Scott and Raven truly felt for each other.

Lydia smiled and greeted everyone, but the minute they were in Scott's private office and the door closed, she collapsed into his chair.

"Oh, I'm so glad that's over! Did I really have to meet everyone all at once? I'll never remember any of their names."

"That doesn't matter," Scott said. "I just want them to know you."

She laughed and slipped her sandals off, tucking her legs underneath her on the chair. Scott watched her. He sat in that chair nearly every day. From now on, he knew would always imagine this when he sat there— her slender legs folding up, her dimpled elbow resting delicately on the armrest, her long ebony braid trailing down the back of the seat. He swallowed and was aware that he was incredibly turned on watching her like this, and from the mischievous gleam in her eyes, she knew exactly what effect she was having on him.

Lydia held out her arms and he melted into them, mouths joining as he pulled her out of the chair and against the wall, pressing against her and feeling the body he dreamed of every night. She took his hands and guided them to her belly. He attempted to slip them lower but she held them still. Scott met her eyes and saw excitement there, and doubt.

"I'm pregnant," she whispered.

Scott went numb. He staggered back, staring at her belly. He had nearly smashed his body against her belly, he realized with shock. What if he had hurt the baby? A baby, he repeated to himself. The reality sunk in and he stared at Lydia.

"When? How long?"

"I found out yesterday," she said shyly. "We— well, it was when we were on the moon together last week. 9 days ago, to be precise."

Scott laughed and some of the worry around Lydia's eyes vanished. Raven's impulsive decision to leave the moon had one good result, at least. Scott studied Lydia's body, glowing and swathed in white, and laid his hands delicately on her stomach, hoping to feel something.

"It's a little early for that," she said dryly. She was smiling, happy.

"We don't have a license," Scott said. "How could you get pregnant without a license? I thought it was impossible. Don't they do something to stop women from conceiving?"

"Not on the moon," Lydia said. "I didn't tell you because— well, I wasn't sure anything would happen. But they want to increase the moon's population so conception isn't limited and getting a license should be easy."

"I can't believe it," Scott whispered. He held Lydia gingerly and felt her warm, soft body beneath his hands. "You're going to be a mother."

"And you'll be a wonderful father," Lydia murmured. "I thought—"

Lydia pulled out of his embrace. She was glowing.

"I know we don't *need* a second father," Lydia continued. "But I thought maybe we could ask Bryce. It would mean a lot to him, I think, to have something in the world that he can love and take care of."

"Yes," Scott said without thinking. His heart felt like it would explode from the overwhelming love and compassion and friendship swelling from within. "I would like that."

Lydia smiled and kissed him gently on the lips. Scott felt moisture on his cheek and realized he was crying. He shut his eyes and pulled her close, inhaling the cinnamon scent of her love and longing to spend eternity in her arms.

Their kiss was interrupted by a beep on Scott's computer; an urgent message had arrived. Scott kept his arm around Lydia while he faced the screen and tilted it to see. Raven, of course. No one else had Scott's private emergency number.

"Speak of the devil," Lydia said slyly. Scott vaguely recognized the religious figure as a quote from an old book, but couldn't quite place it. He tried to open a visual communication but it was text only.

Scott started to write that Lydia was finally earthside and expected a visit from Raven, but Raven sent a three-word message that shocked him to his core: *i need help*. Raven never asked for help, not directly. Scott thought that Raven was secretly terrified that if he ever asked people for help, those people would refuse. Raven's normal reaction to a crisis was to isolate himself, not reach out to others.

i'm in the west

about to be taken by atheus

medane will help

The terseness of the message was nearly as frightening as the content. Scott started to ask if he was all right but the connection was lost. Raven had probably hacked into a computer illegally and couldn't maintain communication. Which meant that he wasn't on his private computer and in serious trouble. The West. Raven was terrified of the Western World, though he had never fully explained why to Scott. He only said that if he ever went to the West, he would be killed.

Lydia's hips shifted against his and he stared at her in surprise, having almost forgotten that she was there in his temporary panic. She pressed his shoulders down and helped him sit in his chair, then started typing at the keyboard.

"Do you know where to find Medane?"

Her voice was even and business-like and Scott loved her.

"No. Government building, probably, but Lydia," Scott's voice drifted off and he stared at her, the woman of his dreams. Raven was his friend and Scott needed to help him, but Lydia was his wife and his future. Lydia had every right in the world to resent Raven's constant interference in Scott's life and if she wanted him to stay, he would.

"You need to go," Lydia said firmly. "You need to make sure he's okay. He promised to see me, after all," she added, her eyes starting to water. "Help him keep that promise."

"Thank you, darling," Scott said, cradling her precious face between his hands and studying her as if he would never see her again.

———

KAELA WAITED AT ATHEUS' side for his permission before she sprinted after Raven. She was terrified by the thought of what her employer would do to punish her for the moon incident. So far, he had done nothing except look at her as if she were a pawn he might sacrifice. He had only told her that Raven was in the West minutes before the small, unchartered plane had settled into the New Chicago wasteland. When Raven's limp form on the ground sprang to life and disabled the two people guarding him, Atheus had simply told her to bring Raven back. He didn't make any threats but she knew what would happen if she failed.

Kaela ran, surprised that Raven had gotten so much of a head start. It was best that she hadn't seen him up close, though. She wasn't sure how she would react when she saw him again. Chasing him was one thing, but she might need to fight him to get him back to Atheus. Kaela thought of Raven leaving with Nalia and knew that she would be able to fight. He was the only man to ever care for her, and he had walked out with another woman.

A few small buildings scattered the abandoned landscape and Raven dashed inside one. Kaela hoped no one else was using the building; most rural areas like this were home to thieves and worse. Not that Raven couldn't handle it. But Atheus would kill her if she brought Raven back injured. And, although she didn't want to admit it, Kaela didn't want Raven to get hurt if she could help him. She tried to keep her anger fresh. He had abandoned her. But he did have reasons, she knew, and Kaela couldn't help but feel sympathy for him now.

She reached the building. Raven had jammed the door, of course. He was probably trying to communicate with someone. There would be a computer of some sort in the building and Raven undoubtedly knew how to get in contact with his friends. Kaela remembered how easily he had manipulated the moon base's security. An aging outpost like this would pose no problems for Raven if he were really determined to get in touch.

She slammed her body against the door and it shuddered, but didn't give. Circling the building, she identified the only other possible exit and waited in a position where she could see everything. He would eventually come out. She had no real desire to hasten their reunion and was content to wait. She didn't even mind if he did manage to contact his friends. There was little they could do to help now that Raven was in Atheus' hands. Or would be, Kaela amended, once she brought Raven to Atheus.

Minutes passed and a siren wailed in the air behind Kaela. Six police cars pulled up around the building. Twelve officers leapt out with stunguns ready as they circled. She approached the person who appeared to be in charge and attempted to explain the situation, but he ignored her and ordered the police to surround the area.

"Dangerous, armed suspect in building," the police officer said. "Hostages suspected."

"He's not armed," Kaela said. "And there aren't any hostages."

The officer gave her a condescending glance. "Look, lady, we're the professionals here. Why don't you go back to whatever you were doing and leave this to us, okay?"

Kaela imagined punching the man in the face, knocking his teeth in and bloodying his nose. She didn't. Instead, she pulled out her United Western World ID and showed it to him. He went pale and started apologizing. It was not as satisfying as punching him, but it had fewer ramifications.

Kaela approached the door to the building, impatiently waving at the police officers all around her to back off. From the way they were carrying their stunguns, they were more likely to hit each other than Raven. She knocked loudly.

"Raven. You're surrounded. Come out."

One of the officers scoffed. They had probably been told that there was a highly dangerous killer inside, and that was true in some respects. But Kaela knew that Raven was also an intelligent person who wanted to avoid conflict. He wouldn't put up a fight if it put other people at risk. Even if those other people were idiot police, she thought in annoyance as she once again told the officers to back off.

The door opened and Raven emerged. Blood stained his bare arms, bruises covered his face, and he held the doorway for support. The anger and hate Kaela had carefully cultivated vanished into concern and she wrapped an arm around his waist and helped him forward. His eyes were dilated and his breathing shallow. The assassins who kidnapped him must have drugged him, and the drug was still very much in effect.

"Open the car door," Kaela ordered the nearest police. She helped Raven into the back seat—he passed out immediately—before taking the keys from the confused officer.

"I'm confiscating your car," she told her. "You'll get it back in a couple of days."

She ignored the outrage that surrounded her. Atheus always warned her against flouting her authority, but he had given her higher permissions than the police for a reason. They had no choice but to accept her decisions and she managed to take a little delight in the fact that she got to steal one of their cars. Ever since the way the police had ignored the attack on her years ago, she had deeply despised them. Stealing a car wasn't much, but Atheus would punish her if she did anything else. She started the engine and looked around. Atheus would be waiting at the airport. She glanced at Raven through the rearview mirror. He was unconscious and lying across the back seat. She longed to stop and check on him, but Atheus would be able to get him to medical care faster than she could.

She hesitated and wondered whether bringing him to Atheus was the best idea. Surely Atheus wouldn't kill Raven. Punish him, maybe. Raven deserved it, though, she thought with a hint of bitterness. Raven had abandoned her to Atheus, now she would do the same to him. Only, she decided, she wouldn't abandon him. Kaela would stay at his side and prove to him that she was strong, capable, and worthy of his trust.

CHAPTER 12

Raven's arm stung and he looked around, wondering where he was. A small room, in a medical building. A white-coated doctor was setting a long needle down and applying pressure to his arm. She must have given him a shot.

"You'll feel better soon," the doctor said encouragingly. "This will clear any of the drugs still in your system. Can you hear me?"

She flashed a light in his eyes and he blinked. "Of course," he said, raising his hand to stop her from doing any more tests. He wasn't interested in feeling better; he needed to get away from Atheus. The doctor snapped the light shut in her hand and turned away, saying he should get some rest. She left, and Raven immediately stood up and went to the computer. He couldn't get any access and he still didn't know if Nalia was safe or not. The assassins had been after Raven only, he knew, but if Nalia had tried to stop them, they wouldn't have hesitated to kill her. He had no real way of knowing what happened. His brief message to Scott didn't even mention Nalia but he didn't have time.

He regretted sending the message. Scott hadn't responded immediately and the connection had been lost, and Raven could think of dozens of possibilities. Most likely, Scott was out of the office. Lydia was supposed to be arriving sometime this week, Raven remembered, and Scott may have been picking her up. Or, and Raven knew deep down that this was probably the case, Scott was sick of coming to Raven's rescue and would ignore the message. Raven took a deep breath. Scott had always helped Raven, and Raven had never done anything but cause trouble. It was presumptuous to think that Scott would drop everything, find Medane, and rescue Raven. But it was the only choice Raven had. The thought of Scott ignoring the message choked in Raven's mind and he couldn't shake the fear that this was the time he would lose Scott, just as he had lost everyone else who loved him.

The door opened and Raven expected the doctor to return, but it was another woman, familiar and reassuring. Despite Raven's fears and his dire situation, he welcomed Kaela with a warm hug and was grateful when she returned the gesture whole-heartedly.

"I'm so glad you're safe," Raven whispered.

"I'm glad you're safe," Kaela retorted, gesturing at his body.

Raven looked down and realized with shock that he was covered in cuts and bruises. The assassins must have beaten him when he was unconscious, Raven thought angrily. Strangely, the pain was nothing compared to the headache he had felt on the plane hours ago. Days ago. No, the bruises would be healed if it were days, he figured. He wondered how much time had passed since he had hard-wired the ancient computer, contacted Scott, and descended into a drug-induced haze.

Raven laid his hand on Kaela's cheek. She looked scared but unharmed, and she seemed glad to see him. He wanted to apologize for leaving her, but he stopped when another person entered the room. The man was older, with nearly Caucasian-white skin and no hair on the top of his head. He was dressed in dark maroon and when he spoke, Raven realized with shock that this was Atheus in his human form.

"Raven," Atheus said. "So glad to see you again. Kaela, leave us."

Kaela held her ground and looked like she was about to refuse until Raven touched her arm and pushed her forward. There was no need for her to stay, especially if she would get in trouble for it. Atheus watched their interaction with interest, like a cat eyeing its prey. The door slid shut behind Kaela and Atheus' attention returned to Raven.

"Are you aware that you are wanted for murder in the United Western World?"

Atheus' question was without preamble and Raven trembled.

"Yes," Raven said quietly.

"Kaela is as well, as you may know," Atheus said, walking closer to Raven. The room was crowded and Raven uncomfortably backed up until he hit the wall. "I'm prepared to offer both of you pardons," Atheus continued. "If you agree to join my service and work for me."

Atheus represented everything that Raven hated about the world: the corruption, the constant and senseless quest for ultimate power, the utter disregard for human life that was becoming more and more common around the world.

Raven let out a scornful laugh. "Join you? I would rather die."

Atheus' fist crashed next to Raven's face. Raven froze. Atheus' sleeve was brushing Raven's cheek, his fist buried deep in the plaster wall. Raven hadn't even seen him move. If Atheus had hit him instead of the wall, he would be dead. He swallowed hard and tried to fight the fear weakening his resolve.

"That will be arranged, if you choose. But are you prepared to throw your life and Kaela's life away? And what of the rogue díamont? Nalia, wasn't it?"

Raven inhaled sharply. He hadn't told anyone that Nalia was a díamont. How did Atheus know?

"I'm willing to spare their lives," Atheus continued. "Now I'm going to ask you one more time. If you refuse, I will kill you, I will kill Kaela, and when I find Nalia I will kill her as well. Do you agree to join my service?"

Raven took a deep breath and tried to think. Joining Atheus' service would be permanent. Atheus would have access to all of Raven's files and his life would be completely at the díamont's mercy, for as long as that life lasted, at least. Raven had never officially joined Medane; he accepted jobs but had never formally sworn loyalty to the United Eastern World. He longed to say no. He wanted to spit in Atheus' face and use his remaining moments of life to try to kill the man. But he would fail, and other people would die. People he cared about. He thought of Kaela waiting outside, probably wondering what they were talking about, with no idea that her life was in danger. He thought of Nalia and hoped she was safe. No matter how safe she was, though, Atheus would find her.

Atheus pulled his fist back and stared at Raven. Raven felt his shoulders tense and his posture stoop. He lowered his eyes. He had no choice.

"Yes," he finally said.

Atheus grinned. Raven flinched as the man's fist came forward but it turned into an open-handed pat on the back as Atheus pulled him close in a mockery of a hug.

"Good," Atheus murmured. "I even have a job for you, to welcome you to my service. The United Western World elections are being held in a month and one of the candidates has promised to rid the world of díamonts if he is elected. The law prevents me from interfering directly, but I'm sure you're capable of removing the threat. Are you, Raven?"

Atheus met his eyes with a hard, callous stare. Raven had never seen anything as inhuman as Atheus' face in that moment. Cold, calculating, remorseless. Raven wondered why Atheus bothered following the laws of the United Western World when he had so clearly violated the Sydney Peace Accord on the moon base.

Raven nodded, more from fear than an understanding of what Atheus was asking. He would have to kill another human, Raven thought with a shudder. And one who probably was a good person. Raven had never killed anyone who hadn't deserved death and he wasn't sure if he would be able to do it, but he knew Kaela and Nalia's lives hung in the balance. He could either kill a stranger or watch his two friends die.

———

NALIA WANDERED through the kitchen like a ghost. She knew her father was worried about her. He had tried talking to her several times but she could never seem to focus on what he was saying. Raven had been gone for two days. Once the shock of witnessing such a gruesome scene passed, Nalia began to feel deeply afraid for Raven. If he hadn't caused the blood in the room, then the blood had to be his. He was injured somewhere and she was responsible for him. It wasn't just because Raven had been captured while in Nalia's employment, nor was it simply because Nalia had been foolish enough to listen to Raven and stand by while he was taken. She was responsible because her first thought when she saw the blood was that Raven had killed someone and she had hated him.

Klaus glanced at her as she walked past the stove and said something. She ignored him and continued into the main room on the first floor. Immediately she was surrounded by people, her friends and allies, but it was different now. She was different and she knew they could sense it because they left a space around her as she walked.

Guilt over her false assumption made her lose her appetite and Nalia barely spoke to anyone. She had condemned Raven, thought of him as the vilest person alive, when really he had been trying to save his life and protect her from harm. He had been trying to help but circumstances beyond his control forced him into a violent situation. Nalia began wondering about the Graveyard Massacre, if perhaps Raven wasn't responsible for the deaths but had tried to help rescue survivors. Raven had witnessed so much death in his life, how could he remain sane? She longed to find him and hold him and apologize and swear to never judge him again, but he was gone.

Nalia stared at the monitor in the main room that had everything they knew about Raven's disappearance. Five people were working on locating him. They had no leads. Nothing appeared in the papers, no police reports, no indication that anything had happened at all. Klaus urged Nalia to keep her focus on the resistance and not get sidetracked finding Raven, but how could she possibly think about fighting the government when Raven was in trouble? Klaus didn't understand, or didn't want to, she knew. He would never forgive Raven for Taurena's death, and now Klaus was blaming Raven for Nalia's depression as well.

One of Nalia's friends spoke to her and she tried to respond normally but the words wouldn't come. She thought about her own march just weeks ago when she had faced Medane and the United Eastern World. If the police had been carrying real guns instead of stunguns, who knew how many would have been killed? Hundreds, probably, and Nalia would have been responsible. One mistake, one miscalculation, and innocent people died. Nalia thought she understood why Raven had left the slums after the massacre. He had done everything in his power to fight for freedom and equality and he had seen his friends murdered around him. Nalia couldn't imagine the horror of seeing an actual body. The blood on the floor upstairs was enough and sometimes she still felt the sticky sensation as she had crawled from under the bed, unaware of what she was touching.

Nalia shivered. She had to find Raven and keep him safe. No wonder he had been awake, no wonder he always looked so exhausted. She didn't want to think about the nightmares that must haunt him. She wanted to be at his side and erase those nightmares. She wanted to hold him and tell him that she finally understood, that she didn't blame him for anything.

Klaus watched her as she left Grader's Inn. She glanced back and wondered if he had any idea where she was going. Nalia had come to the conclusion almost immediately that the only person capable of finding Raven was her archnemesis Medane. She had waited and hoped for two days and couldn't wait anymore. Klaus blew her a kiss and gave a weak smile before returning to the kitchen.

He probably thought she would be back in a few hours, Nalia figured. She had started taking long walks around the neighborhood to clear her mind and look for traces of the getaway vehicle. Klaus wouldn't even realize something was wrong until the evening, when Nalia didn't return, and he probably wouldn't start to really worry for a day or two. Nalia wondered if she would still be alive. Medane would kill her, she had no doubt. The question was whether he would do it before or after Raven was found. But she couldn't be a child anymore. She needed to stand up and take responsibility for the people who followed her.

When Nalia reached the main downtown she took an elevator to the 30th floor and tried to blend in with the people around her. Most looked at her with disgust; her green tank top and pale denim pants stood out starkly from the various shades of gray worn by the business class. She wondered how many of them had even heard of her resistance movement. It was easy to think that everyone in the world knew about the anti-government resisters, but there were so many people. She was a single spot of color in a sea of blank suits and faces.

The government building was open, as always, and Nalia first went to the room where Raven had quit Medane's service. It was empty. Someone must have noticed her and thought her suspicious, however, because as soon as she turned around three armed guards approached. She tried to be polite and asked if she could speak to Medane. The guards smirked and grabbed her arms, roughly escorting her into an elevator. One of the guards, a man, frisked her for weapons with a thoroughness that normally would have shamed Nalia to her core. Today, though, she held back tears and tried to think of Raven and how much he needed her strength.

The elevator opened and Nalia was shoved into a reception area. She wondered if she were going to be imprisoned or if they would actually let her see Medane. It wouldn't be unheard of for the police to lock her up without filing charges and keep her indefinitely. Before she could worry about her fate, and Raven's, a man stepped out of a nearby office. He was about a head taller than her, strongly muscled, with just a few gray hairs. He nodded at her as if in recognition and she realized that he must be Medane. She had only seen Medane in his díamont form and she had never really considered that he must also have a human form.

"I believe the young lady is here to see me," Medane said, extricating Nalia from the guard's tight grips.

He led her into the office and she was grateful to leave the lewd guards, even if she were potentially going somewhere far more dangerous. Medane locked the door and gestured for her to sit, but she was too nervous and remained standing. This was Medane. The díamont who had ended the Last War. The Eastern World's greatest weapon. Symbol of everything she hated about the government. Standing right in front of her, politely waiting for her to speak.

She took a deep breath and thought of Raven. He needed her help, and she needed Medane. When Raven agreed to work for Nalia, he had refused to attack Medane. He had also worked for Medane for years, so there must be some relationship between them. If Medane didn't care about Raven's life, then coming here was a mistake and she wouldn't live to see the sunset. Her eyes watered and her cheeks heated at the thought. She didn't want to die, but she knew what she had to do.

"I need your help," she said, trying to exude confidence and self-assurance. But her voice wavered and Nalia knew she was on the brink of tears. "Raven was hired by me, by the resistance, and he has been kidnapped. I need your help finding him."

Medane crossed to his desk and sat down, tapping his fingers as if deep in thought. "You're sure this isn't just some attempt to distract me while Galley starts another protest?"

Nalia shook her head. Medane hadn't refused, and that gave her hope. She braced herself, hoping that her next words wouldn't be her last. She needed to earn Medane's trust if she wanted his help, and there was only one way to do that, even if it cost Nalia her life. "There won't be a protest, because I am Galley."

CHAPTER 13

I f the situation hadn't been so dire, Medane would have been amused at Raven's cleverness. The boy had promised to bring the díamont to Medane and he had done so when he brought Nalia. Raven had just neglected to mention that Nalia was the díamont. Medane had wondered how Raven could break a promise the way that he had, but now Medane understood that Raven hadn't broken anything, as usual. Honesty and virtue were Raven's most endearing qualities, and were the reason Medane didn't immediately kill the girl.

She was a díamont, yes, but she was also a friend of Raven's. She was here, in Medane's office, putting herself at his mercy in order to ask for help. As much as Medane wanted to kill her or do something to prevent her from leading future attacks, he understood how much of a sacrifice she was making by coming here. She expected death, but she was willing to die if it meant helping Raven. A person capable of that kind of compassion could not turn into a monster like Soren. Especially if Raven was in love with her. Díamont or not, Medane couldn't bring himself to harm someone that Raven held in such high regard. He was not going to kill Nalia.

"Oh, don't worry, I'm expected," a voice said from outside Medane's office before a young man burst in, followed by Medane's flustered assistant. The man looked at Medane curiously and opened his mouth to speak, probably to introduce himself, but he caught sight of Nalia and stopped. The man grinned and approached her instead.

"I see I'm in the right place. You must be Nalia," and he swept up the girl's hand into a kiss. "Raven told me about you."

At the sound of Raven's name, both Nalia and Medane relaxed. Medane gestured for his assistant to leave the room and examined the stranger. Medane recognized him as Raven's friend, although they had never met before. Medane had seen the two of them together several times over the years. The man was older than Raven but his dark brown hair didn't have a trace of gray, and the wrinkles around his eyes were clearly from smiling rather than age. Mid-thirties, perhaps, Medane thought. Old compared to Raven, perhaps, but still a child compared to Medane.

"And you must be Medane," the man said, nodding politely. "My name is Scott. Raven sent me here to ask for your help."

"Whose help?" Nalia asked sharply.

"Well, Medane's help," Scott said. "I don't think he knew you would be here. He's in trouble, he just contacted me."

The girl sniffled and looked to be on the verge of tears. Medane could imagine how much courage it had taken for her to come to him for help, and knowing that Raven had contacted someone else must be heart breaking.

"Where is he?" Medane asked.

"He's in the West. He said Atheus had him. That's all he had time to say," Scott added to Nalia. "I couldn't even respond; it was such a brief message."

Medane let out a deep breath and walked to the front of his desk. The other two watched him and he wondered how far they were willing to go to save Raven. Medane would do anything and if Raven really was in Atheus' hands, there was no choice but to help him. But leaving the Eastern World at a time like this could prove disastrous. The moon had started communications again and tension between the world governments was at an all-time high. Interfering in Atheus' plans now was almost certain to cause a fight, perhaps even a war.

"If we can find Raven and get him to the Canadian embassy in

Quebec," Medane said, "then Atheus won't be able to attack. Atheus cannot know that I've left the East. If he does…"

Medane's voice faded and he thought of Sydney after the first attack of the Last War, of Vancouver, of all the cities destroyed. Surely Atheus wouldn't unleash that kind of devastation just because Medane rescued Raven. No, Medane assured himself, Atheus might have become corrupt, but he would never actually kill people. And once Raven was under Lethe's protection in Quebec, there was nothing Atheus could do to harm him.

"I can leave NeoLondon for a few days, and I can help you locate and rescue Raven," Medane said. The other two looked relieved, although Nalia still seemed to be harboring resentment. Medane didn't blame her and wondered whether or not they would ever be able to trust each other. If he was to leave NeoLondon undefended, however, he needed that trust.

"Will there be attacks on NeoLondon?" he asked Nalia directly.

She looked angry, then frightened, then shook her head. "No. Not if I go with you."

Medane nodded and looked at Scott. "I'm glad Raven has such close friends." He gestured to both Scott and Nalia in an attempt to prevent hurting her feelings more. "We need to leave immediately. We can take my private plane."

He was about to ask if they needed any clothes or supplies when he realized that both Nalia and Scott had come with small backpacks. Clearly they were ready to leave. Medane asked his assistant to gather a few things for him and led them to the landing pad on the top floor. Normally he would ask a pilot to fly them, but he wanted as few people as possible to know about his absence so Medane planned on flying himself.

Hopefully Scott and Nalia could figure out where in the Western World Raven was before they got near the border. Probably in the north hemisphere, close to the United Western World's capital in old Washington DC. They would need to land the plane somewhere out of the way, find Raven, and fly to Quebec before Atheus realized they were in his territory. Otherwise, it would take months or even years to undo the political damage between the world governments.

RAVEN CHECKED the scope on the rifle again and glanced at Kaela. He wasn't sure why Atheus was letting them work together to prepare for the assassination but he wasn't going to complain. Raven had already taken advantage of the computers in the room to send a silent distress signal to Scott, assuming he were looking for it. Scott would need to be nearby, within a hundred miles, before he would be able to detect the signal but it would lead Scott and hopefully Medane straight to Raven's location. Kaela was on the computer now, scanning for the best position to shoot. The candidate would be giving a speech in front of the old White House soon. The area had only low buildings, none more than fifteen stories high, and while security would be heightened for the speech, no one expected an assassination attempt.

"Here's one," Kaela said, pointing to a corner building with a clear shot of where the podium would be.

"I guess that would work."

Kaela must have heard the misery and defeat in his voice because she walked over to him and laid her hands on his shoulders.

"I know it's hard," she said softly. "Gleeman—the candidate—isn't exactly a wonderful guy. He takes bribes like everyone else and he supports the Brazilian militia, which you know has killed over 200 civilians in the past year alone."

Gleeman. Raven had felt better before he knew the man's name. Such a strange name, too, clearly a public name rather than a private one, and not a name one would choose for an assassination target. He knew what Kaela was trying to do and he appreciated it, but it wasn't enough to have her tell him that the man was corrupt. Always before, Raven had physical, incontrovertible evidence proving the wrongdoing of the person he was killing. In every case, there was clear proof that killing this one individual would save the lives of hundreds of others. But Raven had never heard of this Gleeman before and had no way of knowing whether Kaela's words were true.

"You don't want to do this," Kaela said. "I wish you didn't have to."

She glanced around quickly and embraced him, her lips tickling his ear. For a moment he was shocked, wondering what she was doing and how she could possibly think this was appropriate.

"This is a chance to escape," she whispered directly into his ear. Her hand slid through his hair. "Atheus wants us to be together," she added as if in explanation. "You can find a way to escape."

Raven swallowed as Kaela pulled even closer to him. He didn't think she was trying to be seductive but he was having trouble keeping focused as her body slid against his. So Atheus wanted them together? It made sense, in a way. Certainly it explained why Kaela was allowed to be here, and why Atheus seemed so interested in their relationship. Perhaps Atheus thought that if Raven fell in love with Kaela, he would be bound to the Western World just as she was.

"You need to escape too," he murmured. "I won't leave you with Atheus again."

He felt Kaela's head nod against his, her fingers clench as she sighed. Raven stroked her cheek and was surprised to feel tears. "What's wrong?"

"I love you, Raven," she whispered.

Raven inhaled sharply and stared at her. Her eyes were red with tears, the bags under them visible. Her lips were dry and chapped, her cheeks thin. She looked as though she hadn't slept in days. Probably hadn't, he thought. But the honesty and sincerity lighting up her pale brown eyes was stunning. She was beautiful.

Raven kissed her on the lips, tenderly, gently, resisting her attempt to add passion. He loved her. Raven knew it like he had never known anything before. It was as if she were a part of him that had been lost long ago. He loved her, but not the way she loved him. Kaela pulled out of the kiss first, a disappointed look in her eyes.

"I'm sorry, Kaela," Raven said. "I do love you. But not…"

She shook her head and smiled, lifting a hand to wipe away tears. "It's okay. I shouldn't have expected you to— I just thought—"

She took a deep breath and met his eyes with a confident smile. "Friends?"

Raven nodded. "Friends."

He hugged her again, closely, and whispered a location outside of

Baltimore. If she could make it there, he knew he would be able to help her escape. As long as Scott was able to find him in time, Raven thought. He tried not to consider what would happen if Scott had ignored the message or wasn't able to find him. Raven wasn't worried about himself. Atheus probably even expected Raven to attempt to run away after assassinating the candidate. But Atheus wouldn't expect Kaela to run as well, and she was the one Raven was most concerned about.

They both jumped as the door to the room opened and Atheus walked in. He seemed pleased to see them so close together. Raven wondered if he even suspected that Kaela was plotting against him.

"Time for you to leave," Atheus said, indicating the clock. The speech was due to begin in one hour. "You have everything ready, I hope?"

"Yes," Raven said, unable to keep the anger from his voice. Atheus seemed so pleased at the thought of getting rid of a human and Raven was ashamed to be helping him. "I'll take him out and wait five hours before reporting in again."

It was normal to wait before reporting in, although five hours was longer than necessary. Raven would need time to hide from authorities and dispose of the evidence before appearing before Atheus. Atheus said nothing, but Raven knew that he would be closely guarded to prevent him from running away. If Scott had gotten Medane's assistance, then perhaps there was a chance for Raven to escape. But if nothing else, he planned to stall as long as possible to give Kaela enough time to reach Baltimore. She would be able to take care of herself from there even without Raven's help.

Kaela waved at Raven as he left, and he hoped she would have the courage to run. The thought of leaving her with Atheus was horrifying, but her destiny was in her own hands. She could stay or run as she chose. Raven had his own destiny to worry about, and his own escape.

Atheus escorted him out of the building and gave him a few warnings before allowing Raven to leave. Raven immediately took an elevator to the lower levels where there would be fewer people and began making his way to the building Kaela had identified as a good spot. He didn't want to consider how she knew what made a good sniper nest, but he trusted her.

Raven wore black, as usual. He had requested a simple black outfit rather than a military uniform because it would draw less attention. In the United Western World, the only people allowed to wear all black were the executioners who carried out Kaonite judgments. They signed an agreement and were given the right to carry out death sentences, and in exchange they agreed to remain executioners until they died. Any who attempted to quit or leave the business were killed in accordance with Kaonite laws. It was a harsh system but it seemed to work; there were far fewer violent crimes in the West than in the East. Raven was used to being feared in black, but he had never been despised before and he was shocked at the disgust and scorn he saw on people's faces when they caught sight of him. Perhaps a military uniform would have been better.

Raven reached the corner building and used the empty stairs to reach the top. The speech would be given on the tenth floor walkway that passed behind the old White House. The White House itself was dwarfed by its skyscraper neighbors, but locals refused to let it be demolished and replaced with something more modern. Looking down at the square building with its distinctive dome, Raven couldn't understand the attraction. Perhaps it was a Western value that he had missed out on growing up, but seeing the old building didn't fill him with pride or hope or any of the things he had heard people say about the White House. Instead, it filled him with despair, because just behind and above the White House, an innocent man was about to lose his life.

Gleeman stepped up to the podium surrounded by thousands of cheering fans. Raven wished he didn't know the man's name, but he would have learned the name even if Kaela hadn't told him. Huge posters sporting the man's name and likeness were everywhere. Raven winced each time he saw the large face staring at him, watching him, almost daring him to shoot. He focused on the lens and prepared the gun.

The speech started. Raven ignored the words but couldn't ignore the loud shouts of support and loyalty from the crowd. Gleeman was popular. The man's mouth opened and shut in Raven's lens, his hands gesturing boldly and confidently. Raven didn't listen. He knew if he listened, he would see the man as a human and be unable to kill him. Seeing the man through the lens was easier. Gleeman was a collection of parts, not a human. A mouth, hands waving, eyebrows lifting and lowering in an exaggerated and almost inhuman way.

Not a person, just a thing, Raven told himself. He fired.

CHAPTER 14

Nalia was grateful for Scott's comforting presence as they flew over the Atlantic. It was a nice contrast to Medane's cold, emotionless conversation. Medane was interested in finding Raven and leaving quickly. Scott was interested in learning about Nalia and she was more than a little flattered by the attention. He was a charmer, she quickly discovered, able to get a smile even from Medane. Scott explained that he was a reporter and Nalia could see how he would be excellent—he was so interested in everything that it was hard not to reveal information.

Scott and Medane were discussing possible ways of finding Raven in the front of the small plane while Nalia curled up in the luxurious seats behind. She had never been on a private plane before, or even in first class. Her trips to the Asian state were in large planes holding hundreds of people and she had been one of many stuck in the small seats breathing recycled air. She didn't mind at the time, but Nalia knew that she wanted her next flight to be as spacious as this. She stretched her arms and legs, enjoying the wide spaces and soft fabrics of the private plane. She wondered if Raven had flown in this plane before. Probably, she decided. He did work for Medane, after all.

Nalia reached into the small bag she had brought and pulled out

Raven's computer. She had kept it with her at all times since he left, hoping he would attempt to contact her. So far, she hadn't even figured out how to turn it on.

"That's Raven's, isn't it?" Scott asked. She nodded and he sat next to her as if waiting for her to do something with it.

"Um, you can look at it," she said, embarrassed to admit that she didn't know how to work it.

She understood computers, of course. Just not this one. She had tried every single button, every possible switch, and as many combinations as she could think of, but still the screen remained black.

Scott took the computer and held his palm over the screen for a few seconds. The screen blinked on. Nalia couldn't believe it and her surprise must have been evident because Scott patted her shoulder.

"Fingerprint lock," he explained. "I always make him put my prints in his security system just in case. He claims it weakens the security, but it hardly makes a difference whether one or two sets of prints unlock it. I'm sure he'll add you when we find him," he added.

She nodded. She would be happy finding him first. She didn't need access to his personal files. Although if she did have access, she thought, leaning forward to examine the screen, she could find out more about him.

"I think," Scott murmured, fingers racing across the keypad. "Yeah. I can find him with this. Medane."

Scott moved back into the pilot's area and Nalia followed, reluctant to leave Raven's computer and equally reluctant to be near Medane. Scott was explaining something about radio signals and Medane was nodding. They seemed to know exactly what they were doing and she felt completely out of place. Both men were dressed in dark gray with long-sleeved jackets despite the heat, and they looked casual and sophisticated, as if they had rescued Raven a dozen times before. Maybe they had, Nalia thought sadly. She would have no way of knowing. Raven hadn't even asked for her help. She was just a girl who had gotten caught up in the bigger world and she was scared that when Raven saw her out of her element like this, he would dismiss her.

She wanted him to value her and see her as a real person worthy of respect, but what if he kept seeing her as a child who needed protection?

He had been so desperate to keep her safe before he was taken and she had agreed without a fight. Not anymore, though. From now on, she would be the one protecting him. She was a díamont, after all. The experience with the bracelet in her fight with Atheus had frightened her and she hadn't transformed into a díamont since then, but she could. Medane and Scott and even Raven would have to acknowledge her then.

"Nalia," Medane said. She snapped to attention. "We've found Raven. He's somewhere in this building," and he tapped one of the screens displaying a map. "I can land on the roof, but you and Scott need to get Raven back here immediately."

Nalia nodded and was reassured by Scott's hand on her shoulder. She could already imagine Raven waiting for her and she realized that she might actually survive to see her father again. It didn't seem like Medane was going to kill her, and once she found Raven, they would be able to return to the Eastern World in triumph. Klaus wouldn't be thrilled to see Raven, she knew, but he would be glad to see his daughter again. And Klaus would certainly be happy that Nalia had succeeded in something as risky as asking Medane for help.

She thought of her father and realized with surprise that she missed him intensely. She had lived at home with him for over two years and had gotten used to having him nearby. They didn't speak much and often went days without seeing each other, but just having her father nearby was a comfort Nalia hadn't fully appreciated. Now, thousands of miles away and surrounded by strangers, Nalia wished she could be home.

As the plane approached increasingly urban areas, Medane was in constant communication with flight towers, repeating information again and again. He had fake clearance to land in old Washington DC but not anywhere near where Raven was. Still, he was somehow managing to land where Scott said the signal was indicating. Scott was positive that the signal was Raven and he promised that Raven would be looking for them when they arrived. Nalia wondered how he could be so certain. Scott reminded her of her father a little, how he could enter any situation with a level head and complete faith that things would turn out for the best.

"That's it," Scott said as the plane slowed down. Scott opened the exit and Medane lowered the plane towards the roof. The engine groaned at having to maneuver vertically, but it was well within the plane's capabilities.

When the roof was just a few feet below, Scott jumped. He stumbled and fell, but waved for Nalia to come down quickly. She leapt and the shock of landing jarred her shins and knees. She was tempted to adopt her díamont form, but she didn't want to attract attention.

Scott pushed her towards one of the stairways and she glanced back to see him descending another. They only had minutes to find Raven before the police would suspect something unusual about the hovering aircraft. Nalia stopped at each floor, making a quick loop before continuing down. She had no idea what she was looking for, aside from Raven. The building was mostly empty but she ran past two startled women who were carrying baskets of wire stripped from the walls. When she had gone down five stories, she paused and leaned against the stairway. Where was Raven?

She stared down the stairs. Nine more stories. It was possible that Scott had already found Raven and they were waiting for her to return. Raven wouldn't be on a lower level, would he? Nalia shut her eyes and tried to think. Time was important. She could either continue checking even though it was unlikely Raven was below her, or she could return to the plane and hope Scott and Raven were there. She wished Scott had given her clearer instructions on how to look for Raven.

A loud crash from above made Nalia's decision for her; it had to be the sound of fighting. She leapt up the stairs two at a time, ignoring the stitch in her side as she hastened back upstairs. The sounds were coming from the second to top floor and Nalia was surprised to see Scott and Raven backing into the stairway only a few steps above her. She didn't have time to be happy, however, because a man with a gun followed Raven and Scott. He hadn't seen Nalia yet. He had the gun pointed at Raven and he was making some sort of threat. Raven was attempting to reason with him. Nalia saw her chance to protect him and acted without thought.

She transformed into Galley, almost relishing the momentary paralysis that signaled her díamont form. She pushed Raven and Scott to the ground and grabbed the man's gun. He was pale. She squeezed her hand around the gun and it shattered. The man screamed and ran. Nalia was tempted to follow him but the thought of Raven stopped her. She didn't have time to make the man pay; she needed to get Raven to safety.

Still in díamont form, Galley gently lifted Raven and Scott in her arms before racing up the final flight of stairs. They weighed next to nothing and she was delighted to be able to carry them so easily to safety. Medane was still hovering in the plane, but other planes were approaching rapidly. Galley easily lifted the men into the plane but when it came time for her to get in, she was unable to maneuver her bulkier diamond body into the door as the plane started turning. Medane shouted and one of the nearby planes opened fire. Bullets glanced off her diamond skin. She heard Raven cry out and looked up to see a bullet slice through his leg. Galley gathered all of her strength and jumped upwards into the plane, changing back into her human form just as she landed. The plane wobbled but held. She could barely believe that the move had worked. Scott yanked the door closed as more bullets sprayed across the plane, and all three of them fell backwards as Medane pulled the throttle.

Raven pushed aside Scott and Nalia and hobbled to Medane.

"Baltimore safe house," Raven gasped.

"What about it?" Medane asked.

"We have to stop there," Raven said, clutching his leg. "Kaela's there."

KAELA DIDN'T HAVE much trouble leaving the city, not that she expected much. Atheus was focusing on Raven and didn't seem to think her capable of independent action. She was glad; it made escaping that much easier. She just hoped Raven would be able to get out. He had called for help, she knew, but she wasn't sure how Raven's friends would be able to get him out of the middle of Old Washington DC.

Kaela switched cars twice on the way out of the city, taking time to select unmarked, unnoticeable cars each time. As she pulled over a third time to scout for a new ride, she noticed another car stopping. The car had been following her for a few minutes but she hadn't thought it suspicious considering the traffic. Now, though, she was on edge. She climbed the stairs to the 10th floor walkway. Two people had gotten out of the car and were following her up the stairs. She gripped the railing on the stairs and considered her options.

They were undoubtedly Atheus' men hired to keep an eye on her. Technically she wasn't doing anything wrong right now and she had the right to go about her business. They didn't know she was running away. She could continue as she planned, get in another car, keep going, and worry about them later. They would follow but they would have no reason to report anything unusual to Atheus.

If she tried to lose them here, however, they would certainly alert Atheus. She would gain the advantage and make it to safety, but Atheus might tighten his watch on Raven. She wouldn't be able to forgive herself if Raven were trapped with Atheus while she was free. On the other hand, Raven had abandoned her once, trusting her ability to survive. Perhaps she could do the same to him. He was capable, after all, and strong. She smiled as she thought of his arms around her and his lips on hers. He said he loved her. Not completely, not yet, and she understood. There was so much happening in their lives right now, how could anyone expect to form a relationship? But they were friends, and in time, she knew they would become much more. Until Raven was ready to whole-heartedly return her love, she would cherish every moment of their friendship.

She would trust Raven, Kaela thought. He could escape on his own. She didn't need to worry about him anymore.

With that decided, she continued along the walkway, trying to blend in to the crowd. She could still see Atheus' men following her so she climbed to a higher walkway near the heart of Baltimore. She ducked inside a homey looking restaurant serving spaghetti and waited by the door until the men had passed. Hopefully they would think she was just visiting Baltimore for personal reasons and not bother reporting her movements. Even though she thought she had lost them, she kept an eye out as she left the restaurant and found another empty car waiting to be stolen.

Atheus would be able to track her ID as she used them to start the cars illegally, but not for a few days, she hoped. With any luck he would never even think to look for stolen cars when tracking her down. Most people walked or took the train, but the train was too carefully monitored and there was only so far Kaela could get on foot. The car started without problem and she drove off before the owner could notice. Stolen cars were common, and most neighborhoods shared community cars rather than purchasing individual ones, so Kaela didn't feel too guilty about the theft. She wouldn't be damaging the car and it would probably find its way home eventually, after all, so it wasn't really stealing, just borrowing. She knew it wasn't a very sound argument but, as usual, Kaela decided to worry about morality later and focus on survival for now.

Raven had given her the location of a small airfield in the middle of Loch Raven Park. She wondered if he had chosen the location because of the name. Even if she arrived before him, she would still end up with one Raven, Kaela thought with amusement. She left the city and had been driving for only a few minutes when she noticed another car tailing her. This time the police car was marked and she had no doubt she was being followed. The buildings had ended and she was on the edge of the park. Kaela pressed her foot against the accelerator. She was committed to running away. She couldn't give up now.

Kaela unbuckled her seatbelt, keeping one hand on the wheel as she examined the road. There was no way to stop and get out. The trailing police car would catch her. Her best option was to jump from the car while it was moving. If the police saw her leave the car, they would follow but she would have a head start. If they only saw the car crash and didn't realize she wasn't inside, they might waste time searching for her there instead of following her into the woods.

Kaela leapt from the car in a single fluid motion, swinging the door open and rolling out, keeping her head protected as she crashed into the ground. For one horrible moment, she couldn't move. She wondered if she had overestimated her strength, if she had been crippled by the fall. She thought she heard the squeal of metal and the sound of a crash as the car exploded into the forest unguided, but it could have been her own heartbeat thumping in her ears.

She tried to let her body go limp and suddenly she could move again. Kaela staggered up and looked around. Her car was engulfed in flame several hundred yards away and the police car was with it. They hadn't seen her leave, then. She had a few moments before they realized she wasn't inside. Kaela forced her legs to move, first one, then the other, in a painful pattern of walking. She suspected she had broken at least one bone when she hit the ground but she didn't have time to worry about injuries. She needed to get deep into the woods and find Raven.

Kaela stopped every few yards, out of breath and in pain, but kept pushing onward. She was leaving a trail of blood and she was losing blood quickly. Her left arm, she decided, was broken. Bone was exposed and she was bleeding heavily, but she tried not to think of it. She would heal. She had always healed faster than other people, and this would be no exception. Darkness fell as she stumbled through the woods, hoping she was heading in the right direction. She felt light-headed and calm, almost as if she were a spirit traveling toward the afterlife, dragging her body along on a final journey.

She breathed in the resin spiciness of the trees and for a moment imagined she lived in a world where trees grew everywhere, not just in special sanctuaries. They were magnificent creatures and one of the things Kaela had missed most while living on the moon. As she leaned against one of the trees and gathered her strength, she touched the bark and rubbed her palm against the harsh texture. She hadn't seen a tree in over eight years and she longed to wrap her arms around it the way she had when she was a child growing up in old Portland. She paused and stared at the tree dreamily.

Most of Kaela's memories of Portland were fond. She still remembered visiting the small shops on 23rd Avenue and buying her first paper book. There were trees along the avenue, she remembered fondly. Not as large as the trees in this forest, but real, live trees. It was only outside of the metropolis area that Portland became dangerous, as most suburbs were. Anyone with money stayed as close to downtown as possible, and as high off the ground as they could afford.

But she couldn't enjoy the woods, not yet. She was losing blood and in shock, and if she stopped for too long, she would never be able to get up again. She couldn't stop until she was reunited with Raven and the two of them were somewhere safe. She didn't know where; it seemed they would be hunted wherever they went. But she trusted that someday, she and Raven would be able to live in peace. Kaela walked through the woods as the sun set and she listened to the sounds of wild animals and insects buzzing and chittering in the humid air. She felt peaceful, content. The faint buzz of a plane engine signaled the airfield that Raven had told her about and she emerged from the trees in front of an antique wooden cottage.

There, next to the wooden house. It was Raven. Kaela couldn't contain her smile and marveled that she had doubted his ability to escape. Of course he had gotten away, and of course he had come back for her. She stepped into the light of the house and Raven greeted her with a hug. He was favoring his right leg but seemed otherwise fine. She held him tightly for a long moment, not sure whether she was enjoying being in his arms or enjoying the end to her agonizing trek, before looking at the other people with Raven.

A man who must be Raven's friend grabbed her by the waist before she collapsed. She clung to him and saw Medane. Good, she thought wearily. She was glad that Medane had been willing to help rescue Raven. And—Kaela felt the pain return abruptly to her aching body as she recognized Nalia, holding Raven's hand.

CHAPTER 15

Medane lost the police planes halfway to Quebec and suspected that Atheus had called them off. He wasn't sure if Atheus knew that he, Medane, was here, but he certainly knew that Raven was headed to the one place he would be safe. Lethe would not have been forgiving if Atheus had tried to shoot him down while traveling to the Canadian Embassy, the one place where neither Atheus nor Medane had any authority.

Raven was fine; Nalia had helped bandage his leg. She had holed up in the back of the plane with Raven, and Scott was successfully keeping Kaela conscious by asking her about possible attacks from Atheus. They weren't in any serious danger anymore from Atheus, but Kaela was dangerously anemic and desperately needed medical care. Medane knew Scott was keeping her awake because he was afraid once she fell asleep, she would never wake up again.

Keeping Nalia out of the way was also convenient for Medane, who had not yet figured out how to explain to Lethe that she was the rogue díamont. He was hoping Lethe either wouldn't find out, or perhaps that Lethe would be willing to speak to her and get to know her before killing her. Crippling her, at least, Medane thought. Lethe was incapable of killing a human, but Medane was certain that whatever Lethe would do to prevent her from becoming a díamont would inevitably lead to her death.

He still remembered Soren's death vividly. Soren lay on a table in díamont form, tied down and unconscious. He had never been allowed to regain consciousness since the blast destroying London. Medane and Atheus stood nearby, knowing that they would be killed after Soren. Lethe had held out his hand and laid it on Soren's chest, and Soren had screamed in pure agony. Contact with Lethe's skin was instant death to the díamonts. Smoke and heat poured from the table and Soren's body seemed to melt into a pile of ashes before their eyes, the scream lingering long past the face and mouth had decayed into dust. Medane was terrified, but Atheus stepped forward and held out his hand to Lethe.

"If the world is safer without me," Atheus had said, "Then I don't want to live."

Medane still marveled at Atheus' bravery. They had fully expected to die that day, but Atheus' decision to volunteer for death swayed the hearts of the humans watching, and had swayed Lethe. Before Lethe took Atheus' hand to begin the destruction, he stopped. An almost human look of pain flashed across his face, the only expression Medane had ever seen from him. Lethe had looked at both of them—Atheus, proud and prepared to die in order to protect the world, and Medane, terrified but equally prepared—and Lethe spared them.

They would eventually meet Soren's fate, but Lethe had given them valuable time and Medane had used it to cultivate his friendships and learn what it meant to be human. He had thought Atheus was doing the same, but now Medane wondered if Atheus' decision to volunteer for death wasn't a coldly calculated move. It was the only thing Atheus could have done to survive, after all. But it was so sincere at the time. Medane had never questioned Atheus' motives before and he wished he didn't have to now. They were brothers and there was no reason they should be fighting. Medane wished he could reach out to Atheus the way he had as a child and find the friend he knew was hidden somewhere. But Atheus had grown cold, and it was harder and harder to find his friend within the diamond shell.

Medane received a message from Lethe welcoming him when they were still miles away. Lethe knew he was in the West, but did Atheus,

Medane wondered. Lethe was always able to tell where the other díamonts where, some part of his programming, so Atheus didn't necessarily know that the Eastern World was vulnerable right now. Medane sent a message back requesting medical assistance when they landed. Lethe confirmed but made no comment and Medane wondered how to introduce Nalia to him.

Díamonts weren't human and couldn't be human, except possibly for Nalia. Lethe had said she was primarily human. If she had managed to balance her human and díamont instincts safely, then there was a chance Lethe would let her live. Medane was afraid that he was bringing Nalia to her doom by bringing her to the embassy, but he had little choice if Raven and Kaela were to survive.

They landed without incident outside of Quebec and were met by Lethe in person. Kaela and Scott got off the plane first and Kaela was rushed to a stretcher. Medane flipped through the safety checks to turn the engine off, trying to delay the inevitable. Nalia helped Raven off and a doctor immediately took Raven to one side to examine the bullet wound. Medane stepped off the plane just as Nalia reached out to shake Lethe's hand.

"Stop!" Medane cried, leaping forward.

It was too late. A static charge knocked all of them backwards and Nalia went white. Lethe let go of her instantly and backed away. The girl collapsed and Medane rushed to her side. She was breathing; she hadn't dissolved the way Soren had. Medane shut his eyes and held her close. He never would have been able to forgive himself if he had allowed Raven's love to die. She was alive, and Medane let the doctor take his place.

Medane couldn't meet Lethe's gaze as he stood and walked away from the girl. Lethe was watching him impassively, probably trying to decide whether or not to kill both Medane and the girl. Medane approached Lethe until they were nearly touching, closer than they had ever been before in their lives.

"I can explain," Medane said. "You have to trust me. My life is yours, but you must let me explain."

Lethe stared at him, examined the close distance between them, and looked at the girl. She was pale and trembling, clearly in shock. Raven was at her side and even Kaela seemed concerned. Lethe shook his head. Medane braced himself for the touch that would be his last, but Lethe seemed to be thinking to himself, not deciding to kill Medane. Lethe's unlined face, normally a reminder of Medane's own mortality, now appeared young and innocent. Medane glanced at Nalia and wondered if touching her had reawakened human memories in Lethe.

"I don't kill," Lethe said quietly. "I don't want to kill. If you say you have a reason, Medane, then I will listen."

Lethe looked at him and for the first time Medane saw genuine sympathy in his eyes. Medane remembered when Lethe had first opened his eyes. Lethe was designed to be a killer, he had been designed to be ageless and emotionless but once again, Medane saw that the humans had failed in their design. It had never even occurred to Medane that Lethe might not want to kill him or Atheus because of friendship or kinship rather than a calculated cost/benefit analysis. Medane had always viewed Lethe as impartial and impassive, but now he saw that Lethe, like everyone, was just trying to connect with someone else in the world.

"Thank you, Lethe," Medane said. There was nothing else to say.

THE PROCESS of firing nuclear weapons was ridiculously long and convoluted, in Atheus' opinion. He had bribed as many people as possible to make the process smoother, but it still required a few accidental deaths before Atheus had command of the United Western World's remaining nuclear arsenal. Technically the weapons were defunct, but Atheus had spent years carefully reactivating them without Lethe's notice. He had never planned on using them, but he had always known that he needed a backup plan in case Medane turned against him.

Atheus had given Medane every chance in the world to return to NeoLondon and ignore Atheus' quest for power, but Medane continued to interfere. Atheus had expected Medane to track down Raven, though not so soon. He hadn't expected Medane to also take Kaela. Without Kaela, Atheus' plan for creating a race of superhumans couldn't succeed. He was furious that he had given the girl so much freedom. He should have chained her in the deepest prisons in the West to make sure she didn't run away. But she pretended to be so obedient and, like Medane and Lethe, Atheus was not always able to identify human emotions, especially the irrational ones like love.

Perhaps Medane still could, Atheus corrected himself. At one point both Medane and Atheus had experienced life as a human and felt the pain and joy of friendship and betrayal. But as the years stretched on, Atheus had to go to further and further extremes to feel anything aside from resentment at the humans. Atheus still remembered the shock and horror he and Medane had felt when Soren murdered the Catholic Pope on national television and proclaimed that the second coming of Christ had arrived. He declared that Medane and Atheus were the Antichrist and would lead the world into destruction. Atheus had been in tears for days, although it was hard to imagine such a thing now. At the time it had seemed unnecessary and cruel to kill, but now Atheus understood Soren's motivation. He wasn't trying to kill; he was trying to create chaos in order to *feel* again.

That was why Soren attacked Sydney first, Atheus knew. Australia was a strange target with no ability to retaliate, but it was precisely this reason that made it an ideal target to terrify the humans. Atheus couldn't attack as broadly as Soren had in the Last War, but he could still wreak havoc. And when Atheus saw human faces feeling such extreme pain and fear, he could vaguely remember what those emotions felt like himself. A shadow of what had once been. Now that Medane had interfered and given Atheus a reason to attack, Atheus could finally satiate his desire for emotion. He would destroy cities and murder friends, and he would watch their anger and terror and the foolish hope humans always seemed to sustain. He would watch Medane. And maybe, maybe Atheus could feel what it was like to be human one more time.

Atheus knew that part of the reason he wanted to hurt Medane was jealousy that Medane seemed happy in his life. In the isolated quarantine of the Last War, Atheus had held back his tears in order to support the younger, weaker Medane. He had hidden his fears to protect his brother, and somehow in the years that followed, he had never regained the ability to cry. The only fear he now felt was fear that he would die without ever experiencing the richness and potential of life. It was unfair that Medane had so much while Atheus ended up with so little, and he was determined to even the score.

The key, Atheus thought as he stood with his assistant next to the final detonation switch, was knowing what to destroy in order to maximize suffering. Structures could be rebuilt, after all, and Atheus knew that Medane didn't care about the physical well-being of his home. NeoLondon could be razed to the ground but if no one were hurt, Medane would ignore the attack. No, to get Medane's attention and really cause him pain, Atheus needed to target the people. Once Medane saw that the people of NeoLondon were being killed, he would be forced to abandon Raven in Lethe's care. The United Eastern World would be forced to retaliate even without Medane's consent, and war would be inevitable. But at the end of this war, only those loyal to Atheus would remain. If Kaela, Raven, and the new díamont could be persuaded to join him, then he would welcome them. They would give him a vast advantage when controlling the rest of the population. If they refused, they would be killed. Either way, a new world would begin, a world that Atheus could rule forever.

Atheus grinned at the thought. His assistant paled, her hand trembling as she reached for the button to activate the first hydrogen bomb to be detonated in over fifty years. The bomb would explode at a high altitude over NeoLondon in three hours, blocking all communication, destroying any airships flying over, and decimating the city and everyone in it. It was time to begin.

CHAPTER 16

Medane cradled his head in his hands. Ten minutes. That was all the warning the people of NeoLondon had gotten. Enough time to transfer all of the sensitive files to the backup computers in Seoul, enough time to cower behind the thick steel support beams and hope the radiation passed them by, but not enough time to escape. Atheus had paired the hydrogen bomb with traditional bombs and NeoLondon was a shattered mess of half-standing buildings and scattered corpses. Perhaps a few people at the edge of the blast zone had heard the siren, recognized it, and made it to safety. But the nearly 19 million people who called NeoLondon their home were gone or would be soon.

The bomb had been detonated midair to maximize the casualties. Structurally there would have been minimal damage without the traditional bombs. Most of the buildings could withstand an indirect nuclear blast, or at least the buildings farther from the epicenter could. From what Medane could tell, the bomb had been detonated at the center of Díamont Crater. It was as clear a message as he had ever seen. He had crossed Atheus, and now Atheus was starting an all-out war against him.

Medane had no idea how Lethe would react to the news. Earth's atomic weapons were supposed to be deactivated, although both world governments had kept a few. Just in case this happened, Medane thought grimly. How would the United Eastern World react? Normally he could predict the president's actions, but the president was dead, killed in the blast. With the president dead, power reverted to each nation-state until a new president could be elected, and with each nation acting alone there was a good chance the entire Eastern World would descend into chaos and civil war. Exactly what Atheus would want. There had to be some way to avoid it.

He knew he was focusing on the politics to avoid thinking of the real human casualties. When he told the others, each had reacted differently but all had been stricken with grief. It was Raven's grief that Medane worried about the most, however. He knew Raven would blame himself for the attack and consider all of the millions of deaths a direct result of his action. If he didn't do something to pull Raven out of his depression, the man might never recover.

Medane knew how powerfully Raven reacted to each murder that he committed, even the murders that Raven approved of, and he knew that Raven still mourned the people killed in the Graveyard Massacre even if he didn't speak of it. The NeoLondon bombing might be enough to push him off the edge and Medane would do anything to prevent that. It might also be enough to send his superhuman abilities into overdrive. Perhaps that was one of the reasons Atheus had chosen NeoLondon as his target; he knew it had special significance for Raven as well as for Medane. Killing two birds with one stone.

He typed frantically as he attempted to reach all of the world leaders and talk them out of instant retaliation. Africa was willing to wait for an Eastern World Conference to discuss possible retaliation, but India and Europe were pushing for a quick strike against the Western World. They were also putting forth candidates for the open position of president. Medane warned them not to jump ahead in the procedure. He had his own candidate, if Raven was up to the task.

All of the world leaders respected Raven and almost all had worked with him in the past. Raven didn't realize it, but Medane had been grooming him for power for years. He would have liked longer to work out Raven's rough edges, but there wasn't time for that anymore. He would have to promote Raven as a candidate for president and hope that

Raven understood the good that he could do in that position. Everyone else being promoted was corrupt with power, like the old president; Raven would bring enlightened equality and serve the ideals that the Eastern World was founded on. If Raven was able to recover from this devastating blow, and if he was the same person afterwards, that was. Medane finished communicating with the leaders and took a deep breath. He needed to talk to Raven and the others before he returned to the Eastern World to sort out this mess.

He found Raven sitting outside the embassy building but still clearly on its grounds, a good move. If he so much as set foot outside of the embassy, there was a good chance Atheus would snatch him up. After all, if Atheus was bombing NeoLondon, he would be willing to kidnap Raven from right under Lethe's nose. But luckily fear of Lethe was still preventing Atheus from entering the embassy itself, so Raven and the others were safe for now.

Raven was alone and had his eyes closed, but he was clearly alert because his head turned when Medane approached. It was rare to find Raven off guard; Medane had never seen Raven truly relax before ever since the first time they had met, when Medane had found the boy sobbing over the bodies of his parents and their murderer. Medane was visiting Portland at the time, having been tipped off by one of Atheus' men that an attack on the superhuman subjects was about to take place. Medane never would have guessed that the attack was on the parents, not the child, and the goal of the attack was to supercharge the child's abilities.

When Medane had arrived, Bryce was covered in blood, sitting over his parents' bodies and weeping. He was holding a gun—his father's, according to the police—and the body of the attacker lay on the floor with a single bullet wound between his eyes. One shot had been fired, and it had been fatal. The attacker was a pro, a hired assassin, no real loss in the world, but because of Kaonite law Bryce was considered a murderer and was due to be put to death. Medane had helped the boy escape and set him up with a family in a wealthy district of NeoLondon.

But Bryce, being the type of stubborn, idealistic boy that he was, had run away from his family and joined the rebellion. Medane had kept an eye on him all his life, though Raven didn't know it, and after the Graveyard Massacre, Medane had finally seen his chance to reunite with the boy. It took years, but eventually Raven joined Medane and Medane had been able to protect Raven properly.

Medane examined Raven's bullet wound and a strange anger bubbled to the surface. No one should be allowed to hurt Raven. Then he met Raven's eyes and when he saw the pain there, he knew Raven would have suffered a hundred bullets if it meant saving a single person in NeoLondon.

"Shouldn't you be returning to your nation?" Raven asked emotionlessly.

"Our nation," Medane corrected, not wanting Raven to distance himself too far even while understanding the instinct to run from the pain. "And yes, I'll be leaving in a few hours. I wanted to talk to you."

"So talk."

"Raven, you are not to blame for this. Atheus has been waiting for an excuse to do this for years. I was blind not to see it before. This is my fault, not yours."

Raven shook his head. "He attacked because I ran, because you helped me run."

"He attacked because I interfered with his plans, yes. You had nothing to do with it."

"But all those people," his voice shook. "Who will mourn them? Who will bury them? Who will make sure this doesn't happen again?"

Medane let out a sigh of relief. Those were good questions to ask. The other leaders were asking who would avenge their deaths, and how many of the enemy should die before they were even. The other leaders were as bloodthirsty as Atheus. There had been no war in decades and they were itching for one, but Raven was not. Raven wanted peace. He would be a good leader for the people. He considered telling Raven his plan, but bit his tongue at the last minute. Raven was too deep in his grief to see his way out. But he didn't seem lost, as he had been after the Graveyard Massacre. That tragedy had completely undone him. This seemed like a setback, but he had friends and confidence to see him through. He would recover, and he would be a formidable president.

Scott slammed back a drink, feeling the burn wash down his throat into his belly. It made no difference. He held the glass loosely in his hand and was vaguely surprised when Medane filled it for him. He knocked it back again, and again the drink did nothing to dull his mind. All he could think about was his wife.

"Have you heard anything?" Medane asked.

"Nothing. She was on a shuttle headed out, but there's no news if she reached the moon or if—if she was caught in the blast."

Not just Lydia, he thought with a sinking heart. Their child as well. Unnamed, ungendered, undeveloped, but their child nonetheless. Having a child was such a privilege in this world, and it wasn't right that it should be taken away so soon. And Lydia. Beautiful, angelic Lydia, helpless in the mesh seatbelt as the shuttle would have been rocked by the initial blast, then incinerated in the sky. Or perhaps the bomb had only shorted out the shuttle and she had fallen to her death, prey to gravity's inevitable pull. What were the chances that she was far enough away? No one knew. The shuttle wasn't due to reach the moon for another day, and Scott knew he wouldn't survive the wait sober.

"Scott, I need your help," Medane said. "The Eastern World wants to retaliate and I need to stop them."

"They should retaliate! Don't you understand what they just did? We have to show them that we aren't afraid, that we won't sit back and take it!"

"No," Medane corrected. "We have to show them that we aren't like them. A new president has to be appointed, and I want to put Raven forward as a candidate."

Scott laughed. Raven, with his black past? But Medane seemed serious, so Scott thought about it. Raven was incredibly careful that none of his activities led back to him. He was the subject of numerous rumors, but police had never been able to pin anything to him except for whatever had happened in the Western World. But there were so many rumors. People were terrified of Raven. It would never work.

"You'd have to nominate him as Bryce, and that opens up whatever problems he has here in the West."

"I can get around that," Medane said. "But I want you to start floating the idea around in your circles, get people talking about him.

Start a popular movement. I can persuade most of the leaders, but he'll need popular support as well."

Scott tipped his head back. Lydia would want it. She would want Bryce in charge of something, in a position to finally do all the good he was capable of. But it meant schmoozing with politicians at a time when he was worrying about—and perhaps mourning—his wife. Was he up to the task?

Medane poured him another drink, then put the bottle away. "Last drink. Think about it. I leave in two hours to return to the East. I want you with me."

Scott sipped his drink this time and nodded, thinking of Lydia and the way her face had glowed when she mentioned asking Bryce to be their second father. The way her eyes had filled with concern and she had sent him away without a second thought when Bryce asked for help. She would do anything for Bryce, and so would he. He put the half-empty drink to one side and stood up. The floor tilted slightly beneath his feet, but it was stable enough. Lydia, he thought as the grey walls blurred in front of him. I'll do this for Lydia.

CHAPTER 17

Pausing in front of a mirror, Lethe stared at himself and frowned. Ever since the contact with the renegade díamont, he had been feeling strange. Raising a hand tentatively to push back his hair, he stared into his ebony eyes, struggling to find some hint of the conflict that he felt. But there was nothing, only the impassive face he had grown to resent.

Perhaps killing Atheus and Medane earlier would have solved everything. Watching the humans and their distress at the news of NeoLondon's destruction, he remembered all too well the previous war and its repercussions. At the end of the war, he had met with the two surviving díamonts to kill them. And had failed.

I'm designed to kill the díamonts, he thought angrily. All of them. Why did I let them live?

Atheus had stepped forward to be killed, and Medane waited patiently. Both of them, so willing, so accepting of their fate. They all knew the horror that the díamonts could cause, all knew the consequences of remaining alive. But Lethe had hesitated. Because when he opened his eyes for the first time, Medane and Atheus had been the first faces he saw. Created with almost no human DNA, Lethe had been born full-grown, and hadn't changed at all in the forty-seven years he had been alive. Awakening as if from a long sleep, their faces had smiled on him. They had been overjoyed, and relieved, to have someone able to end the life of their enemy.

Killing Soren was a gruesome task, and Lethe feared repeating it. The agony and pain as Lethe's DNA worked through Soren's body, destroying the non-human elements, had terrified him. But Atheus had smiled, and held out his hand, waiting for the touch that would end his life so horrifically. Lethe refused. Couldn't kill them, these men he had grown to know. Couldn't destroy the only two people who understood what it was like.

Maybe he could have stopped this war. Maybe the humans would have shown restraint, and the violent tendencies inherent in being a díamont wouldn't have taken another city full of souls. Now, Lethe was torn. He longed to kill Medane while he was still here, and then find Atheus. The humans, though, had changed his mind.

Medane was helping them fight against Atheus, and doing his best to stop the war. His self-control would fail in the end, as it had for all of the other díamonts. But in the meantime, perhaps leaving him alive would help. The girl was another problem. He had been designed to kill díamonts, but didn't have it in his power to kill her. She wouldn't survive long, he knew, not after his touch had jumpstarted the process already at work within her due to the bracelet, but was he required to kill her as well?

She posed such an interesting problem, and he didn't know how to treat her. If she survived long enough to have children, then by leaving her alive, he was neglecting his responsibilities. Lethe frowned as he remembered the file he had forced out of Atheus when the bodies of the girl's mother and brother were found. An infant male had died in child-birth along with his mother, his body encased in diamond. No one knew that the girl existed, and Lethe had studied the remaining bodies impassively, searching for some explanation.

From what he could tell, the liquid diamond that had been mixed with the mother's DNA had fixed on the X-chromosome. The son, having only one X-chromosome, had received too much liquid diamond, and his body had solidified. The other child, Nalia, who no one knew existed at the time, had been born with one normal X-chromosome to balance out the díamont genes, and survived. Her díamont abilities were sex-linked, but would be passed to her offspring.

Females born with the trait would carry it as a recessive, not showing any díamont tendencies but having the possibility of passing it on to their children. If any of Nalia's descendants intermarried, the genes could rise to dominance and a new díamont might be born. The danger was nearer than her eventual descendants, however. If Nalia had a son, he would turn out a complete díamont, more like Lethe and the others than Nalia was herself.

The estrogen produced by Nalia's body seemed to repress many of the violent tendencies that plagued the male díamonts, but any sons of hers would have the full range of díamont powers and the potential to start yet another war. The danger of leaving her alive was balanced against the potential good she could accomplish, and Lethe hesitated, unable to decide.

He wandered the halls until he caught a glimpse of her, dark hair curling around her shoulders and falling over her back. She saw him and smiled. He asked her to join him and entered a private conference room with a torn heart. Her eyes were open and innocent, and her smile was pure.

"Thank you for keeping us safe here," she said, and his indecision increased.

"You're welcome," he said haltingly, and turned his back to her as he shut the door. There was so much energy inside of her, so much of that strange aura he associated with being human. Her touch had awakened distant memories in him, memories of a time of peace. She was only barely a díamont, but still capable of wreaking the same havoc as the true ones.

"Are you going to kill me?" she asked.

He whirled to face her. Still smiling, holding her hand out to him. She had felt his touch, knew what extended contact with him would do to her, and yet she was giving him the chance. Just like Atheus.

"If you do kill me," her voice wavered, "will that help? I don't know what to do anymore. I don't know how the world can possibly go back to normal. If you think this would help, then do it."

She moved closer to him, and he lowered his eyes. Would it help? She was so young, so innocent. She posed no threat, and it was hard to imagine her ever turning out like Soren, or Atheus. Killing the díamonts wouldn't stop the violence. She was a leader among her people. If he left her alive, perhaps she could gather everyone together and start a new world order. Maybe this time it would work. If she lived long enough. Already the bracelet's poison was at work within her, changing and mutating her DNA, slowly destroying her. The effects weren't visible yet, but they would be soon.

"No," he said. "I'm not going to kill you. You're needed here."

"For what?" she asked, and he was struck by the pain and bitterness in her tone.

"Because people look up to you. People trust you. You have a chance to start over and heal the world. Are you really going to turn it down?"

His mouth tasted acrid at the lie, but he ignored the feelings of guilt that threatened to choke him. Would she survive long enough to accomplish that? Somehow, he doubted it, but she needed his assurances right now.

Nalia nodded and returned to the others, and Lethe lifted a trembling hand to his forehead. Would he regret this act of mercy, as he regretted sparing the others' lives? It had been so easy before, when all he had to do was make sure that neither Atheus nor Medane grew too powerful. They balanced each other, both too afraid to kill the other, both aware that Lethe wouldn't allow only one of them alive. Now, though, it was time for Atheus to die. He had gone too far.

NALIA TWIRLED the bracelet around her wrist as she entered the room where Raven was staying. He was alone and his eyes looked red; she knew he would never let anyone see him crying. Her mind was still whirling with her conversation with Lethe, and with Medane. Both of them thought of her as a leader, and they expected her to do something to stop the violence. But she was still so young, barely a child. She wasn't ready for this. She still depended on her father for so much, and her father—

She shook her head sharply to keep from thinking of her father. There was a chance the slums hadn't been hit as hard as the main city. There was a chance her father had survived, and her friends. Not much of a chance, but it was all she had to hold on to. That, and Raven.

He reached a hand out to her and she took it without a word. Her own eyes were red with crying, she knew, and Raven cradled her in his arms without speaking. The feel of him against her body sent her pulse racing and she cursed her baser impulses. How could she be thinking about him like this when the whole world was falling apart? But she was intimately aware of his breath upon her cheek, his hands stroking her back, his steady breathing and firm heartbeat. She was aware of him in a way she had never been of anyone else. She looked up at him and saw a strange expression on his face, as if he were torn between sadness and desire just like her. She closed her eyes and tilted her face towards his, pursing her lips and pressing against him.

He laid his lips upon hers and she marveled at how smooth his lips were. She had never kissed anyone that she cared about like this before. At first all she felt was the physical sensation—not unpleasant, and what she was expecting. Then his hand slid across her back and he pulled her tight, kissing her in earnest as ripples of pleasure extended outward from the kiss. It was just like she had dreamed kissing him would be like, only under very different circumstances.

She tried to ignore that last thought, but it was too late. The thought of her father lying dead somewhere, rotting and unburied, swarmed through her mind and she pulled out of the kiss with a sob. Raven kept her close and kissed her neck.

"I know," he whispered. "We'll find a way to honor them. We won't ever forget them. Their sacrifice will not be in vain."

She held him tightly and let the tears come, needing him desperately in this moment of weakness. Had he felt the same after the Graveyard Massacre? Had he spent his life trying to honor and remember the victims? And how could they possibly honor an entire city of millions of people? It was too big a task for her, too big for anyone. Medane thought she could help; he wanted her to return to NeoLondon to find survivors and revitalize the rebellion, only he wanted her to persuade the rebellion to join forces with the government against the Western threat. He seemed to think that she had the power to change all of their minds. But she was so young. Sure, she was a díamont, but she had only made her grand entrance weeks ago and very few people outside of NeoLondon knew who she really was.

Nalia wanted to stay with Raven. Raven couldn't leave the embassy, and more than anything she wanted to stay. But Medane needed her help and she knew, deep down, that she could do it. It terrified her to take over where her father left off, but she knew it was her destiny to lead the rebellion no matter what happened and she would make sure that the rebellion stayed intact even after the devastation of NeoLondon. She would make sure that the rebellion stayed loyal to Raven after Raven became the new president, even if it meant that the rebellion had to make concessions to the government. She had always thought of the rebellion as something clear cut—either you were with the rebellion or you were corrupt—but now she was beginning to see that there were good people in the government, good people who had just been massacred partly because of her actions.

Raven rocked her gently and kept kissing her head, her neck, and finally her lips again. She let him, and when they kissed a second time the memories of her father faded and she tried to focus on the present, not the past or the future. She didn't know for sure when she would see Raven again if she went with Medane. This might be their last few hours together, and she wanted to make them last forever.

"Are you going with Medane?" he asked.

"I think so."

"You should. You can do a lot of good talking to your people. They need a leader."

"That's what Medane said."

Raven smiled, and cupped her cheek in his hand. She managed a smile as well.

"If I go—you'll be here when I get back? You'll stay safe?"

"No one's letting me leave," Raven said with a bite of anger in his voice. "I don't have a choice."

"But promise me you'll stay safe."

A haunted look crossed Raven's face. "I broke a promise today," he whispered. "I promised Lydia I would see her, and now we don't even know if she's alive."

Nalia stroked his face and kissed him. "I just don't want to lose you, too," she said. "I don't think I could survive."

They kissed again, and soon all of her thoughts vanished except for thoughts of him beside her. Raven pushed her backwards on the bed until they were lying beside each other. A flush of heat went through Nalia's body as Raven began pulling off her shirt. Was he going to do what she thought he was doing? She wanted it, certainly, but she felt extremely inexperienced. She hesitantly helped him pull off her shirt, then his, and they lay together as he stroked her body and the only thing she could think of was him, right next to her, and how much she wanted him.

He caressed her body while they kissed, and his hand tangled in her jeans as he undid the button. She flinched in anticipation but he must have misinterpreted the movement because he stopped.

"Sorry," she whispered. "Keep going."

She normally had little shame about her body, but she was shy about showing herself and she was grateful that he was still kissing her and not looking at her. She reached over and turned off the light, giving herself a little more privacy. Then she realized that she couldn't see his body, and she very much wanted to. Instead of turning the light back on, though, she began exploring him with her hands.

Raven's body was mostly smooth and strong, with hard muscle and almost no fat, but he had several scars across his back and arms. She knew his leg was still bandaged from the gunshot wound and made a mental note to go slowly when she removed his pants. She wanted to ask about the scars, but her body was on fire and this was not the time for talking. She wanted action. Her fingers stumbled over the buttons on his pants and he had to help her as he undressed. Although she was curious about what he looked like, she still didn't turn the light on because she didn't want him looking at her too closely.

They kissed again, and then Raven straddled her. He kissed her and the world turned to pleasure. With her arms wrapped around his neck, she barely felt him enter her, but she did feel when he began to move. They writhed together in a sinuous rhythm, until Nalia began to moan and Raven groaned over her. Everything turned to bliss and he relaxed against her, cradling her in his arms.

Nalia felt spent and exhausted, but it was as if some sort of valve had been released and her emotions had finally been drained. Her fear and panic were gone, for the moment, and all she felt was happiness and love. She drew Raven close to her and breathed in the musky scent of him for a long time.

They would have stayed like that for longer except for a knock at the door, and Medane's voice informing them that Nalia needed to be prepared to leave in ten minutes. She reluctantly sat up and again the only thing she wanted was to stay with Raven. But she had responsibilities, and she now knew that Raven would be here waiting for her. There was no room for mystery or miscalculation in their relationship anymore: he loved her and she loved him. They would end up together, she knew it.

She went to the bathroom and cleaned up, then they switched places and she got dressed. She would have preferred to take a shower, but time was pressing. She hoped Medane and Scott didn't guess what she and Raven had been doing. Once she was dressed she turned the light on, just as Raven came out of the bathroom wearing nothing. To her surprise, he looked embarrassed and tried to cover himself. Apparently she wasn't the only one unused to being naked around others. She politely didn't look, aside from a quick peek. He was beautiful.

He pulled on a pair of pants and seemed to regain his confidence with the clothing. She kissed him.

"Goodbye for now," she said. "But only for now."

He stroked her cheek and kissed her forehead.

"I love you," he whispered. "Goodbye."

CHAPTER 18

Scott took a deep breath before he finally left the aerostation. Medane and Nalia had dropped him off at Paris before continuing on to NeoLondon, and the city had a panicked look to it as people rushed about their ordinary lives. No one knew whether there would be a second attack, so even the normal traffic had a frantic air as people went about their business and prayed it wouldn't be their last action. Scott knew that a lot of the people were staying home, or traveling to be with loved ones. A war was starting and even though life continued, everyone had learned about the Last War and knew how war could topple governments and the status quo in a matter of days. Grabbing a cab, he went the housing complex of one of his friends. Taking the elevator to the 14th floor, he rang the doorbell and ran a hand through his hair.

He looked reasonably presentable, he knew. Medane had lent him a suit, since all he had brought was casual clothing, and the suit—though indisputably nicer than any in Scott's usual wardrobe—hung on him slightly and didn't quite fit right. It looked like he had found it at a discount shop and that took away from the niceness of the suit. Still, he was grateful for Medane's thoughtfulness. It was likely that all of Scott's belongings had been destroyed in the attack on NeoLondon. Not that material possessions mattered much. He was still waiting to hear from the moon to see if Lydia's shuttle had made it out safely.

The door opened to reveal an elderly man, wide belly neatly tucked into a clean suit. His pale grey eyes widened at Scott's sudden appearance and the man welcomed him in.

"Scott, old friend," he said. "I thought..."

"No, I wasn't in NeoLondon," he answered the unspoken question.

"What a relief!" the man exclaimed. "I'm so glad that you're here! Er," he paused. "Why are you here?"

"You've probably noticed that another world war has started," Scott said. At the man's shock, however, he frowned. "It hasn't been announced? Do you have somewhere I could write up a story?"

His friend pulled up a chair and computer as his wife strolled into the room, staring down her nose at Scott's ill-fitting attire. He swept up her hand, planting a kiss on it.

"Madame Alma," he murmured, watching her look of shock turn to pleasure.

"Scott! I almost didn't recognize you! What's happened?"

"Quite a bit, really. If you want to hear about it, you'll have to wait though, this needs to get written."

The man nodded his approval. "Your paper knows where it's at, really. Can't believe the courage it must've taken, letting the world know about that bomb only minutes before it went off. Yes," he continued, oblivious to Scott's sudden inhalation. "You reporters have a noble calling."

"What happened?"

"That editor of yours, Sandra something. Instead of finding a spot to hide from the radiation, she wrote up a beautiful story warning the world what was happening and sent it out. Dedication, that's what it is."

Scott stared at the ground. He knew from Medane that the people of NeoLondon had about ten minutes warning, and Medane was hoping that there were survivors because of those precious minutes. Had his paper helped? Had Sandra's sacrifice saved lives? At the very least it seemed to have alerted the world to what was going on, although it was shocking that his friend didn't think another world war had started. NeoLondon had just been bombed; how could a war not be starting? He took a deep breath and thought of all the times he had hassled Sandra about his stories and deadlines. He had secretly hoped she would still be alive. If she was dead, then what chance was there that Lydia was alive?

Alma glanced apologetically at Scott, and dragged her husband into another room. "We'll be in here when you're done," she said.

He nodded his thanks, and started writing. John and his wife were ideal starting places, due to their connections in high society. Once he had their support, he could get a strong network of people to help support Medane and, ultimately, Raven. Medane's plan to propose Raven—Bryce—as the new president was a good one, but it would require quite a bit of legwork so that people were willing to accept him despite his reputation.

He couldn't help but check on the status of the moon shuttle, but once again it was undetermined. He cursed. Surely the shuttle was in contact with the moon, even if it hadn't docked. The only reason they wouldn't know at this point was if the shuttle was destroyed, but even though he was bracing for that reality, he still wasn't quite sure how he would react. Lydia couldn't be dead, she just couldn't be. She was his world.

Scott took another deep breath and pushed the shuttle out of his mind. He was going to try his best to make sure that when the war ended, not only would Atheus be defeated, but the world would elect a new leader to lead them out of the chaos. That leader would be Raven.

THE CITY WAS GONE. Nalia stared out the window in shock as they flew over what used to be NeoLondon. Crumbling wrecks, scattered spires reaching a floor or two before giving in to gravity, everything had been leveled. Medane was absolutely still when they flew over the city to drop her off at the slums, and Nalia wondered how he felt. He had lived through the Last War, after all, and had seen scenes like this before, even right here in NeoLondon. What was it like seeing his worst nightmares come to life again? Despite herself, she felt sympathy for him and she knew her task of persuading the rebels to side with Medane until the war was over would be slightly easier now that she herself believed in it. He would never let this devastation happen anywhere else, not if the grief on his face was honest.

After being dropped off in the middle of a desolated street that Medane said showed plenty of heat signatures and that she vaguely recognized as her home, she had wandered to Grader's Inn to find her father. She was stopped on the way by a pack of rebels, armed and confused. They were all young, and bore signs of the bombing in the blisters and sores covering their bodies, not quite hidden by the layers of filthy clothing they had wrapped themselves in. Nalia shuddered. It looked like a scene from a horror vid.

"Who are you?" the eldest demanded, a woman that Nalia vaguely recognized as Jess, one of her friends before the attack.

Jess wore a scarf that covered most of her face but couldn't hide her lack of hair or the open sore running across her right cheek. It looked as though she had found partial protection from the worst of the radiation. Nalia had worried about the radiation, but Medane had assured her that díamonts didn't suffer from radiation poisoning and they would be safe. His goal, he said, was to locate survivors and get them to medical care while her goal was to revive the rebellion and convince the rebels not only to move out of NeoLondon but also to support Medane in this new war.

"It's me, Nalia."

"Nalia is dead. Prove your identity or die."

Nalia tried to think of some way to prove her identity when the most obvious solution popped into her head. She would transform into a díamont. She wasn't wearing any metal so there was no risk, and no one else could possibly transform. She shut her eyes and felt the familiar paralysis that always frightened her, then she opened her eyes. Jess and the others were cowering in fear.

"I told you, it's me. I'm not here to hurt you."

"You sided with Medane," Jess accused. "That's how you escaped the blast."

"No," Nalia said, already seeing how difficult her job was going to be. How could she persuade them to join with the government in this conflict if they thought the government caused the bomb in the first place? "Where is my father?"

Jess hesitated. "He's gone."

Nalia transformed out of her díamont form abruptly. "What do you mean, gone? Did he try to follow me? Where is he?"

In her heart she already knew the answer. He was dead, and it was confirmed by the sudden sympathy she saw in Jess and the other rebels. Her father was dead, and all because she had chased after a man. He had warned her about Bryce, warned her that Bryce was trouble, but she hadn't listened. She had run to Medane, the enemy, and persuaded Medane to find Bryce, and now NeoLondon was razed and her father was dead. It was all her fault.

She dropped to her knees and was aware of Jess putting a comforting hand on her shoulder. All of the energy seemed to flow out of her body. The bracelet seemed to tighten uncomfortably around her wrist and she could feel every vein in her body, as if her very blood were boiling. Her father was dead. Nothing could bring him back. She had run away without saying anything, even goodbye. Now she would never see him again. She collapsed on the ground.

"Nalia," she heard Jess say. "Are you alright? What's wrong?"

But she couldn't respond. Her body was locked; her vocal chords boiling with her blood. Her father, gone. Permanently. She thought of Raven and the precious moments they had shared together. Was it worth losing her father? She didn't know. All she knew was that she would never see her father again, and her body was shutting down. Something was seriously wrong.

CHAPTER 19

Raven paced the embassy, angry and frustrated. Kaela was still here, trapped like him because of the threat from Atheus, but the others had all left. He had heard nothing from them. Nothing. Not even whether or not Lydia was alive. He was forbidden from accessing any computers and the guards who followed him every minute of the day were strict enough that he couldn't even get close to a monitor. Kaela was under looser surveillance, he knew, and he resented her for it. She could find out about Lydia and the others, but she didn't.

He thought about losing his guards, but he knew that Atheus was nearby and undoubtedly had people stationed just outside the embassy, waiting for Raven to do exactly that. He would put up with the surveillance if it meant being protected from Atheus, but there was only so much running he could do. He hadn't yet told anyone that he had agreed to serve Atheus. The shame of the memory still ran deep. He thought of how Medane would look away in disappointment, how Nalia would draw back in disgust. At times it felt as though he were branded with Atheus's mark and he wondered that no one noticed. As long as Atheus was alive, he was a slave.

As he paced, he caught sight of Kaela and her entourage. She looked up at him hopefully, but he was in too foul a mood to be nice.

"What are you up to?" she asked.

"Absolutely nothing," he snapped.

He regretted his harsh tone instantly as she withdrew and seemed to close up. She was under just as much stress as him, he reminded himself. He had no right to be cruel to her.

"I'm sorry," he said. "It's just this place."

"I know." She toed the ground. "It's not just this place, it's this life. I didn't ask to be this way. I just wanted a normal, ordinary life, but instead I'm stuck here, trapped here, because of something that I didn't have any control over. It isn't fair."

Raven reached out to touch her shoulder and she leapt away from his touch.

"I don't want your pity," she said. "People are dead because of me."

"You think you're alone in that? We're all responsible. And in case you hadn't noticed, I'm trapped here too."

"Yeah, but you chose your life."

Raven thought back to his childhood, to the murder that had determined the rest of his life. He didn't even remember it, although he thought about it so much that he had created false memories of it. Killing the man who killed his parents and earning the death penalty under Kaonism. No, he had not chosen his life. He had been forced into it because he grew up running, always running. Even though the officer who helped smuggle him out of the West found him a good home, he always felt like the government was out to get him and he had run to the rebellion, the only place free of government control. The only place where his past didn't matter.

But it did matter, and he realized with a shock that he had never told Nalia about it. She had slept with him not knowing the most basic fact about him: that he was a killer. She must have known, he reasoned. She knew the rumors, she saw the room after he was taken by the kidnappers. She knew he killed people. But she didn't know how young he was when he made his first kill.

Kaela watched him with something like pity in her eyes, and he held his hand out to her. She took it. He knew she wanted more out of the relationship, but he was only prepared to give friendship. Still, there was no harm in a hug under these trying conditions. She held him tightly and her body trembled. He knew she was trying to keep back tears. She probably didn't want to cry in front of the guards. He had already done his crying after Nalia left. She was the only pure, joyous thing in his life and she was gone.

One of the guards stepped forward and placed his hand on Raven's shoulder. Raven was shocked; they were there for protection, not to interfere with anything he did. The guard's hand dropped to Raven's side and then the guard backed up. None of the other guards seemed to have noticed anything, or if they did they didn't react. Raven glanced at his side and saw a note in his pocket. He took Kaela's hand and led her to his private room, the only place the guards weren't allowed. There were no electronics and no exits at all, not even vents or windows, so Raven was considered safe when he was inside.

Once the door was closed, he read the note. Then he read it again, his mind and hands numb with fear.

Nalia will die unless you meet with me. Seattle Center. I will be waiting. Atheus

Kaela took the note from him and gasped.

"How did you get this? That guard? He must work for Atheus. We have to tell Lethe. We're not safe here anymore."

"Nalia's not safe," Raven whispered. "I have to get to Seattle."

"You're not actually going to do this, are you? It's a trap, it's obviously a trap."

"But Nalia—"

"We don't even know if she's in danger. At least find that out before you run off."

Raven hesitated. She made a good point. It was foolish to go into a trap without knowing all of the information beforehand. He would speak with Lethe and see if Nalia was in danger. Lethe had been avoiding him lately, but he would track the díamont down and force answers out of him. If there was any truth to Atheus's threat, Raven would run away in an instant to try to save his Nalia.

MEDANE ENTERED the slums in díamont form and scanned for life. There were plenty of survivors in the buildings, but none came out into the street. He longed to collect the survivors and get them proper medical attention, but he knew they would resist. These were not the grateful survivors from the center of NeoLondon. These were rebels, who thought any government interference—even much needed medical aid—had strings attached. He had come with doctors who waited near the helicopters hoping survivors would emerge and ask for help, but he had little hope any would avail themselves. The people of the slums were proud people, and hated the government with a fury that he had never understood.

He went to the largest concentration of people without hesitation. Surely Nalia would be there. He had received an unusual request from Lethe. Raven had been asking about Nalia. Since there was no communication in the slums, he had to go in person to make sure that she was all right. He wasn't sure why Raven was so concerned, but he was glad that the boy cared about her so much. Raven had shown no signs of interest in anyone else his entire life, always pushing people away rather than inviting them in, but Nalia was different.

Perhaps it was because they were so similar, Medane thought. Nalia was like a younger version of Raven, before he had fallen prey to the cynicism that corrupted the world. She represented the pure idealism that had once been Raven's best quality, and being around her was bringing that quality to the surface in him. Medane was grateful; he had watched Raven's slide into corruption with a great deal of doubt and guilt. He knew he was responsible for most of it, especially since he had tried to bribe Raven to capture the díamont. He wanted Raven to be free and independent, but the world—and Atheus—didn't allow for it, so Medane had chained him down and watched as Raven slowly grew to accept his limitations. Nalia was good for him.

Kaela would have been good for him, too, Medane thought, but not in the same way. Kaela had accepted her gilded cage and she would have encouraged Raven to do the same. Perhaps it was better that Raven had chosen Nalia over Kaela, even if it meant the end of the superhuman experiment.

As Medane reached the building with the highest concentration of people, a survivor stepped outside to face him. He admired her courage. She wore a scarf to cover her injuries but it was obvious she hadn't found shelter in time. She, like most of the people in the slums who mistrusted the government, hadn't paid attention to the sirens warning the people of the impending nuclear strike. She was just lucky to be far enough from the epicenter to be alive.

"What do you want?"

"I'm here to check on Nalia. I have a message from Raven."

He didn't have a message, but he added the last because he thought it would help him get in easier. He knew Raven had a long and confusing history with the rebellion, but he had been helping the rebellion at the end and surely mentioning him would be to Medane's advantage.

"What did you do to her?"

Medane paused. "Is something wrong with her?"

Raven's request began to take on a new meaning. Did Raven know something about Nalia that no one else did? Did he know that something had happened to her? Was that why Raven had forced Lethe to ask Medane about her?

"You can come in, but only if you help my people."

"Of course," Medane said. "I have doctors and supplies at my heli-copters."

At least some good would come of this, he thought as he followed the woman into the dark building. Power was out, he thought idly as he pushed past bleeding and festering individuals to a back room. It must have been due to the traditional bombs Atheus had dropped, because the nuclear blast didn't affect most of the power in the downtown district. It had been eerie walking through the empty streets while pre-programmed ads ran along the buildings beside him, but the traditional bombs had hit the outlying areas and it was no surprise power was out here.

No one was in the room except for Nalia, lying on a cot white as death. Medane dropped to his knee beside her and reached for her hand, then realized he was in díamont form. He wouldn't be able to feel her pulse.

"I need a few minutes alone with her," he said.

"No. I stay here."

Medane silently cursed. He did not want to be vulnerable with a rebel standing by, but he needed to transform in order to assess Nalia's condition. With a grimace, he became a human and heard the woman gasp. She made no move to kill him, however. He held Nalia's wrist and counted her heartbeats. Too slow. She was cold to the touch, but not dead.

Oddly, her body seemed to heat up the closer he got to her wrist, or at least the wrist with the bracelet. Almost as if the bracelet were causing the illness. He touched the bracelet and a shock ran through him as the metal hungrily licked through him, desperate for him. He pulled away quickly. It was definitely the bracelet, he decided. The bracelet must have been designed to destroy díamont DNA, just like Lethe did. If Medane touched it for long enough, he would die. Nalia was lasting longer because she had less díamont DNA, but it was still stealing her life and wreaking havoc on her body. How could he possibly stop it?

He nursed the hand that had touched the bracelet and realized it was scorched and blistering, like the survivors. The woman was looking at him oddly, or perhaps it was just that the usual hate in her eyes was gone.

"Are you alright?" she asked.

"Yes. I need to get her better medical care immediately."

"She doesn't leave."

Medane stared at the woman, then shrugged. There was probably nothing his doctors could do, and if keeping Nalia here kept the rebels happy, so be it. He was more concerned with how to relay this information to Raven without setting the boy into action. Who knew what Raven would do if he found out that his love was near to death and there was unlikely to be a cure?

CHAPTER 20

"What do you think you're doing?"

Kaela entered the parking garage just in time to see Raven finish breaking into a car. She sauntered up to him, trying to look casual, but her heart was pounding. It had taken all of her skill to lose her guards and she knew there was only a short time to convince Raven to take her with him before the guards found them.

"I'm going to find a cure for Nalia. Atheus knows something, I just know it. I have to meet with him."

He got in the driver's side and started the engine.

"I'm going with you," she said, getting in the other side of the car that had automatically unlocked. "You'd better leave soon if you don't want them to stop us."

"You can't come. It's too dangerous."

"Not too dangerous for you."

Raven appeared torn, and she understood why. He was going because he loved Nalia and he would do anything for her. What he didn't understand was that Kaela loved him in a way she loved no one else, and she would not let him walk into danger alone. Perhaps he didn't love her the way she loved him, but she loved him just the same. She would not let him face Atheus alone. No one should be alone.

Raven put the car into reverse and pulled out, accepting her into his runaway plan. Not a moment too soon, because she saw shadows approaching in the garage. She knew they wouldn't try to stop them once they reached the edge of the embassy. The guards were for their protection, a courtesy, and if Raven and Kaela wanted to ditch that courtesy there was little Lethe could do. It wasn't a military base, after all.

The car was an old fuel-cell but it looked like it had enough fuel to reach Seattle. Driving at full speed with minimal stops, they ought to reach the abandoned city in three days. She knew Raven would be sticking to the public highways rather than the more protected roads because he wanted speed, and she didn't think any of Atheus's people would try to stop them on the way. If she offered to drive while he slept, they might even get there sooner. She shivered at the thought of going into Seattle, so close to her old home in Portland.

Seattle was a ghost town ever since the Last War. After the atomic bomb struck Vancouver, in Canada, a massive earthquake had destabilized Mount Rainier and sent torrents of mud down into Seattle, completely destroying much of the downtown and killing thousands of people. A few people still lived there, but it was a shadow of its former self. The only thing that still remained of old Seattle was the Space Needle, a small bulwark against time and nature that stood in an abandoned field of twisted metal and abandoned buildings. Sometimes kids from Kaela's high school would go up to Seattle on a dare and see who could last the longest standing in the field at night, when the ghosts were said to roam. She had never gone. It seemed disrespectful, somehow. And now they would be going to the dead city to meet with Atheus and see if there was any way to save Nalia's life.

Kaela looked over at Raven. His face was drawn as he stared at the road ahead of him, and his knuckles were white on the steering wheel. For his sake, she hoped Nalia recovered. But if the girl did die, perhaps there would be a time when Raven turned to her. After all, they had gotten so close. Just for a moment, but there had been a connection between them that couldn't be mistaken. She knew it was love, but he seemed to shy away from it. Kaela had never connected with anyone before, certainly not since she had killed the man in Portland, and she would do anything to feel that connection again.

"Kaela," he said. "There's an old laptop in the back of this car. Can you get it and check on the moon shuttle?"

"There probably won't be any news," she said. "I checked earlier today. But I'll try."

She twisted in the seat and retrieved the computer, getting to the internet quickly and going to the page she had been visiting for the last several days. It wasn't the public moon page that had the shuttle status displayed; this was the private page for administrators only. She had some perks after working on the moon base for so many years. The shuttle had been injured in the blast but had survived into space. Now it was just a question of whether it could reach the space station in time. Other shuttles had been sent to retrieve the passengers, but the docking equipment had been blown away along with the communication. There was no way to know who was on board, if anyone, and no way to retrieve them. They would just have to wait until the shuttle crashed onto the moon and could be safely evacuated, but that wouldn't happen for another week at the shuttle's current speed.

She related all of this to Raven, whose hands tensed on the steering wheel.

"So no idea if there are survivors?"

"None. The outside of the shuttle is smashed pretty bad, but the inside might be completely untouched. We build our shuttles to withstand a lot."

"How many people know about this?"

"Only a few. To everyone else, it just looks like the shuttle is still in an undetermined state."

"I have to tell Scott. He'll be worried."

"Do you want me to drive for a while?"

Raven hesitated, as if wondering if he could trust her or not. She didn't know what he thought she would do, exactly. She couldn't turn him in to Atheus since he was on his way to Atheus, and she wouldn't return him to Lethe since she would be in just as much trouble. Finally, he nodded and pulled the car over. They switched places and she pulled back onto the road, accelerating until she hit the same speed he had been driving.

"Why don't you sleep, too? I'll drive as long as I can, and then you can take over. That way we won't have to stop."

"Are you sure?"

Again, suspicion tainted his voice and cut into her heart. How could he possibly doubt her when she was sacrificing everything to be with him?

"Yeah. We'll get there a lot faster, and the sooner this is over, the better."

He agreed, and then his fingers began flying over the keyboard. She remembered how easily he had broken into the moon base and wondered what other information he was hacking into while he spoke with his friend. His face slowly relaxed as he typed, and then he sighed and leaned back.

"If you're sure you don't mind..."

"Not at all," she said, pleased when he closed his eyes and leaned his seat back.

It was nice knowing that he felt safe enough to sleep around her, and she couldn't help but gaze over at him occasionally as he slept. After a while, his breathing evened out and she knew he was truly asleep. She kept driving into the afternoon sky, wondering what horrors Atheus had in store for them when they reached old Seattle.

MEDANE SAT at his desk and tried to remain calm. He knew Raven was about to do something impulsive. He had seen that reckless look on Raven's face too many times in the past not to recognize it. He just hoped Kaela could stop him from leaving the embassy, because once he left the embassy, there was nothing anyone could do to protect him. The girl's condition worried him as well, especially since Lethe didn't seem surprised to find out that she was in a coma. Lethe seemed to know about her condition just as Raven had, and it troubled Medane.

The monitor before him snapped back to life and he composed himself as the African minister appeared on the screen. The people of Africa were responding to the attack on NeoLondon with panic, since many of their cities had been destroyed in the Last War, and Medane knew this man was exerting all of his considerable influence to maintain peace and keep the government functioning without a president to make final decisions. It was amazing how little the people trusted their ministers and how much they trusted the president, even when the president lived thousands of miles away.

"Medane," the man said, his voice graveled and heavy with strain. "We find your course of action and choice of appointee acceptable. You have our vote."

Medane nodded and they spoke for a time of the troubles in Africa, and whether or not an appearance by the díamont could make a difference and put an end to some of the in-fighting going on. Inwardly he was celebrating. Africa had agreed to stop the retaliatory strikes and they were prepared to accept Raven as the new president. It was a major victory. He already had China and Australia on board, and now he just needed the rest of Asia to persuade Europe to follow suit.

He was most concerned now with the retaliation—Europe had independently attacked Los Angeles, a once-bustling metropolis that was now abandoned like most of the cities in old California. The heat and rising water level pushed most people inland, but a few remained and they had suffered the consequences of that decision when Europe attacked. They had also bombed old Seattle, more as a message than anything else since no one lived there.

At least they were holding back from attacking the major cities, Medane thought. If they attacked Portland, there would be millions of deaths. Instead they were choosing low casualty targets, as if to show the Western World that while they meant business, they had restraint. So far, Atheus and the West had not struck again, but Medane knew it was only a matter of time. Soon, the entire world would be under siege again, only this time it wouldn't be Soren against the humans, it would be díamont against díamont with the humans as innocent bystanders. The thought sickened him.

With Africa taken care of, Medane took his private jet to the slums to see how Nalia was doing. He tried to visit her every day, despite the danger. He entered and left in díamont form but when he sat with her, he was in human form. Surprisingly, the rebels were beginning to warm to him, perhaps because of his persistence in making sure their leader was surviving.

They were also taking advantage of the doctors and medicine he brought each time and he was grateful. Most of them had only suffered thermal burns and minimal radiation, since the wind had been going in a different direction that day. It was the firestorms that had done the most damage. But a few had been close enough to suffer radiation poisoning and they were beginning to show signs beyond constant vomiting and hair loss. They would have died if they didn't receive medical care. He still hadn't convinced them to leave NeoLondon, where everything quivered with radioactivity, but at least they were getting help.

When he arrived, Jess showed him into Nalia's room as usual. And as usual, she was white as a corpse and he had to change to a human to make sure she was still alive. She was, but it seemed like she was deteriorating rapidly. He looked at his own hand, still scarred from where he had touched the bracelet. If a simple touch had done that to him, he couldn't imagine what it was doing to her. Yet she looked untouched. Whatever chaos the bracelet was wreaking on her insides, it wasn't visible to the naked eye.

"Why do you come here?" Jess asked.

"To make sure she's alive."

"Why?"

Medane sighed. "She is a friend of my friend. That makes her my friend, and I protect my friends."

Jess was silent, then she left the room. It was the first time they had left him alone with Nalia. He stroked Nalia's hair, careful to keep a safe distance from the bracelet. Then he became aware of talking outside the room. He quieted his breathing and could just make it out.

"I don't like him coming here."

"We don't have a choice. He's here to help her and if he cares that much, I'm not going to stop him. Besides, I don't think we could stop him if he really wanted to get in."

"It still isn't right for him to be here. He's our enemy."

"He was our enemy," a new voice said. "I'm starting to wonder if we can afford that."

"Giving in to his demands?"

"No, just considering the possibility that maybe he does want to help Nalia. And if he wants to help her, maybe he'll help us. Maybe, instead of fighting him right now, we should be helping him."

There was a long silence as Medane stroked Nalia's forehead. This was exactly what he wanted, exactly why he had sent Nalia back to the rebellion. He wanted them to realize that he wasn't the enemy—at least, not the current enemy—so that they would side with him in the world war and not distract him while he fought Atheus. But he never would have sent Nalia here if he knew the cost. Gaining the rebels was not worth losing Nalia, not by a long shot. Not if she was Raven's love, and her illness pushed him to do something reckless or insane as Medane suspected was the case. He just prayed the boy didn't get himself killed.

CHAPTER 21

The moon kept a pitiless watch over the night as Raven entered the old Seattle Center. The city had seemed dark as they drove up, speeding through the night, and when they came closer the reason for that darkness had become apparent. Seattle had been bombed, and recently. The old Space Needle, once the only remnant of the great city, now lay shattered on the ground. Raven leapt over the debris as he went to the center of the field, on the lookout for Atheus. He didn't know exactly where to find the díamont, but this was the most likely place.

Kaela waited in the car, or at least Raven had instructed her to. He suspected he would need to make a hasty exit and she was an ideal getaway driver. He just hoped she didn't try to join in the battle. He could reason with Atheus on his own. He examined the area, and then the moonlight glinted off something crimson and the díamont appeared at the center of the crater where the base of the Space Needle still stood. Atheus.

The sight of him filled Raven with rage and he practically flew down to the base, forgetting all of his careful plans about staying emotionless and not showing how much Nalia's life meant to him.

"You bastard," Raven cried. "What did you do to her?"

"Nothing," Atheus said with a feral grin. "She did it all to herself."

"What's wrong with her?" Raven's voice dropped, growing cold and deadly. Most men shuddered when they heard him speak like this because they knew death was near, but Atheus just looked amused.

"That bracelet she's wearing. My people made it, of course, on the moon. It was supposed to end up with Medane, but this is so much better, don't you think?"

He laughed and Raven grit his teeth. The urge to attack was unbearably strong but he couldn't fight Atheus yet. He had been shocked and horrified to learn that Nalia was in a coma, and he wasn't leaving until he learned how to reverse it.

"It finds DNA bonded with díamont elements," Atheus explained, "and tears it apart. On a real díamont, death would follow rapidly, but she's mostly human. She's lasted quite a while. As it destroys the DNA, a lot of energy is created and released in the form of a light wave. Well, a gamma ray actually, quite capable of killing everything within miles when fully unleashed. She's managed to control it so far, but when it kills her," he paused. "She'll manage to take out most of Europe with her."

Raven's heart shuddered in his breast and he took a deep breath. He remembered the light that had shot out of Galley's hand in the fight with Atheus so long ago. He had assumed it was a laser, but she had passed out right afterward. Was she dying even then? He bit his lip until he felt blood, but he had to resist the urge to fight until he knew the cure.

"There's only one solution," Atheus said, clearly enjoying Raven's reaction. "The bracelet can only be taken off by a díamont. A true díamont," he added with relish. "Medane would be able to take it off her, but unfortunately, it will kill him."

Atheus laughed as Raven drew away from him. A true díamont... Medane. It was the only solution. Atheus would never remove the bracelet and Lethe probably couldn't and wouldn't. Only Medane could do it, but that would leave the world defenseless against Atheus's attacks.

"So glad you've decided to rejoin my service, Raven," Atheus said. "I look forward to you doing my bidding in this matter and ridding the world of Medane once and for all."

Something snapped inside of Raven. He would never do this monster's bidding. There had to be another way.

"Never, you bastard. I don't give a damn, I'll never help you!"

The smile on Atheus's face faded. "Then you've killed her, and signed your own death warrant."

Raven took a deep breath. Nalia, he thought. Nalia, I'm sorry. But if he wins, he'll kill us all anyway.

He narrowed his eyes and tried to look as confident as possible. "So be it."

Atheus scowled and leapt forward, one fist raised. Raven barely moved out of the way in time and stared in shock as Atheus's fist slammed into the ground less than an inch from his face and continued into the ground. If he had been there, he would be dead. Raven scrambled backwards as Atheus advanced. Raven braced himself, then charged. He topped Atheus over but the díamont struck him in the side and his ribs cracked. None of his blows made a dent in the diamond sheath covering the díamont, and he realized that he was doomed to lose this fight, but he would go down fighting.

Raven heard his name and look up in shock to see Kaela silhouetted against the edge of the crater. Atheus drew a gun and fired it at her without a second thought. Her eyes widened and in an instant, the world seemed to slow around Raven. He saw the bullet traveling through the air towards Kaela and knew she would be unable to dodge it. But he seemed to exist in a place where he could move faster than the bullet— he knew that if he tried, he could push her out of the way before the bullet struck her. He ran and it felt as though his body was trudging through water but he kept going, knowing it was a race between him and the bullet to reach Kaela. He reached her an instant before the bullet and as he pushed her aside, the bullet tore through his belly.

He collapsed to the ground and everything sped up. The low murmuring he had been hearing became a scream, Kaela's scream, and she was over him, pressing against his wound. Atheus stared at the place where he had been and where he was now with an amazed expression on his face.

"So that is what the superhumans can do," he said. "Too bad it won't save your lives."

He approached them and Kaela stood up, placing herself between him and Atheus. He moaned, the shock of moving so fast combining with the blood loss to make him limp and unable to fight. She looked back at him with inexpressible sadness on her face, but he was unable to indicate that he was still able to fight. His body felt frozen and beyond his control as blood seeped from the wound, and he fell into shock.

Kaela lunged at Atheus, who sparred with her almost playfully. She kept looking over at him as if trying to determine if he were dead or alive, and she called his name over and over with heart-wrenching pain until he realized that she thought he was dead. There was no way to indicate to her that he was alive, just unable to move. She must feel like the only person left alive in the world, he thought, and tears brimmed in his eyes. But she was too far away to see them. Atheus laughed at her and continued to parry her blows like a fully-armored cat playing with a baby mouse. She stood no chance. Raven tried to sit up, to move, to speak, to do anything to tell Kaela that she was not alone in the world when Atheus struck.

His fist slammed through her chest and reappeared out of her back and she stared down at his bloody forearm in shock. She managed to say Raven's name one last time as blood began to pour from her mouth. Atheus pulled his arm out of her and pushed her limp and dying body to the ground. Raven was screaming, even though no sound escaped his mouth. Kaela was dead. No one could survive a blow like that. Atheus had ripped through her heart.

Then he heard footsteps approaching him and for a moment, he remembered his childhood, hearing footsteps just like this after he had found his parents murdered. The murderer had approached him with heavy footsteps just like this, and he had killed the murderer. The footsteps were the same, but his body was limp and useless. He would not be killing Atheus today.

Atheus stood over him as he waited for the blow that would end his life. His parents were dead, Kaela was dead, Nalia was dying, and now he would be dead too. He shut his eyes and braced for the worst, but it didn't come.

"Poor Raven," Atheus said in a mocking tone. Raven opened his eyes and saw the díamont leaning over him. "Lost your little friend, and the díamont's going to die as well."

He raised a foot over Raven's head and Raven flinched, trying to prepare himself for the pain, but instead there was a gust of air as Atheus moved away.

"No," Atheus said, his breath quickening as if in anticipation. "No, I think it's best if you live to enjoy this. When I've won this war, I'll come looking for you. I'll make you beg for mercy."

Raven shuddered as Atheus turned his back and left. His eyes blurred and for a moment it looked like two díamonts were striding out of the ashes of Seattle. As soon as Atheus left, he managed to crawl to Kaela. Her lifeless eyes stared back at him as if in accusation and he shut them, then kissed her blood-spattered face. She deserved better, in life and in death. She didn't deserve to be alone.

MEDANE PICKED up the distress signal a little before six in the morning and within an hour, he had arranged for people to retrieve Raven from the ruins of Seattle. Ever since the boy had escaped Lethe two days ago, he had been on high alert because he knew if anything happened, Raven would likely turn to him for help. And he had, luckily. Raven must have set up some sort of emergency distress call specifically designed to be picked up by Medane because no one else heard anything, but Medane had found it instantly on his computer and knew right where to send the backups. He hated that he couldn't go in person to rescue Raven, but it was only a five-hour flight. The boy was due to arrive any minute, and then the real trouble would begin.

Medane had convinced the rebels to reposition themselves outside of NeoLondon, finally, and they had taken Nalia with them. Visiting her was not as easy as it was before, but Medane still made daily trips into the rebel camp. They accepted him now and no one ever spoke about fighting him. Instead, they were prepared to follow him during the war; exactly what he had wanted. But when Raven showed up, he would undoubtedly want to see Nalia and Medane wasn't sure Raven would still be capable of leading the world if Nalia died. It seemed inevitable that the girl would eventually lose the battle and give in to the bracelet since there didn't seem to be a cure, and her loss would be especially hard if Raven had also just lost Kaela, as Medane suspected was the case. After all, both Kaela and Raven had fled Lethe's protection, and now only Raven needed rescuing.

A brief alarm sounded and Medane went outside to the makeshift aerostation. He and what was left of the government were still stationed near NeoLondon in one of the buildings that had survived, and all ships had to land in the field nearby. This ship would be carrying Raven and Medane would be able to assess the damage.

As Raven limped out of the ship, helped by a young medic, Medane knew his face became an impassive mask. He had to hide the deep concern he felt as he saw the still-bleeding bandages on Raven's waist and the heavy bruising on the man's face and other visible surfaces. It almost looked as though Raven had been caught in Seattle's bombing, although that was impossible. Medane stepped forward and gripped Raven's arm, and the man returned the grip with a grateful sigh.

"You're still alive," Raven said.

"Of course," Medane said, surprised by the comment. There was only one thing that could kill a díamont, and Lethe seemed content to let him live for now.

"I want to see Nalia."

"Let me get you medical attention first—"

"No," he said. "They fixed me up on the ship. I need to see her now."

Medane nodded, seeing the stubborn look in Raven's eyes. He escorted Raven towards the rebel camp, noticing that despite Raven's attempts to walk on his own, he was leaning quite heavily on the díamont. Raven was in bad shape.

"Why did you run away, Raven?"

"He knew the cure," Raven replied. "But it doesn't matter. I just need to see her, I need to know."

"You're not going to like what you see."

"I don't care."

They reached the camp and were surrounded by rebels, all curious to see Raven in the flesh after all of Medane's talk of how Raven would be their new president. He didn't look as impressive as Medane would have liked, but perhaps it was better this way. He certainly had their sympathy. Medane could feel the shock in Raven's body as the rebels appeared and realized he should have warned the man about the radiation and burns that covered most of the people here. They were a shock to see for anyone, especially someone who blamed himself for the attack. But Raven seemed to take it all in stride and once they neared the tent that held Nalia, all of his attention focused on her.

She looked like an angel, or a creature out of a fairy tale: pale, beautiful, and unmarked save for the burn marks that were starting to appear around the bracelet. Her eyes were shut and her breathing steady, but occasionally her eyes would flicker as if she were caught in some nightmare. Raven pushed Medane away and staggered to her side. He pressed his lips against hers as if thinking a kiss would wake her up, but nothing could wake her from the sleep she was in now. Even if the bracelet could be removed, it was possible that enough damage had been done so that she would never survive.

Raven wept at her side for a long time, and Medane kept the rebels away to give him privacy. He never mentioned if Atheus told him a cure, Medane realized after a while. Perhaps Atheus had told him, but it was too horrific. Maybe cutting off her arm, but no, Raven wouldn't weep if the solution were so easy. He grit his teeth and cursed Raven's closeness. Now of all times Raven should be sharing information, not keeping secrets, but the boy still must think of Medane as the enemy even after all of their long years together, even after Medane had done everything and risked everything to save him. Whatever the cure was, Medane was determined to find out before Raven did something else rash.

Still, watching the boy weep over Nalia, his heart softened and he couldn't help but remember Raven weeping over his parents so long ago. Raven didn't know that it was Medane who had rescued him all those years ago; he thought it was a random police officer. And Medane would never tell him otherwise. But Medane loved Raven like a son, and he would do anything in his power if it meant saving Nalia and protecting Raven.

After several hours, he noticed that Raven was trying to pull off the bracelet and failing. So Raven knew about the bracelet. The boy seemed despondent when he couldn't remove the bracelet, and Medane realized that Atheus must have told him that removing it was the only way to save her. But there was no way to remove it, not unless—

The pieces snapped together perfectly in Medane's head. The only way to remove it was for another díamont to take it, and the only other díamont was Medane. No wonder Raven didn't want to talk to him about the cure. The boy must not want to ask him for such a sacrifice, either because he was afraid Medane would refuse, or perhaps because he was afraid Medane would accept and then the world would be at the mercy of Atheus.

The bracelet had plummeted down from above, landing mere feet from Medane's feet. For the first time, he realized that he had been the intended target. After all, he would have picked it up if Nalia hadn't snatched it first. He would have died almost instantly, and Atheus would have been left to rule the world.

Atheus's plan was ruthless, but it had worked. Now Raven had to choose between his love and the man who had helped him, the man who was the string holding the Eastern World together. But not for long. Soon, Raven would be that string and the nations would follow him, and Medane could safely take the bracelet and save Nalia's life. He just needed a little more time.

CHAPTER 22

Raven rested on a cot next to Nalia's, but he didn't sleep. He had been at her side for nearly twenty-four hours now and knew that nothing would wake her up except for killing Medane. If he were younger, the solution would have been simple. Just trick Medane into touching the bracelet and then get Medane somewhere where the resulting explosion wouldn't kill Nalia and the others. But he was more mature now, and knew that killing Medane would have far-reaching consequences that he couldn't even begin to imagine. Medane held the United Eastern World together and he was the reason the various leaders didn't descend into civil war or worse. The president had a lot of power, but only the strength of the díamont ensured cooperation.

And Medane meant something to Raven, which he hadn't fully realized before. He cared for Medane. Medane had been protecting him for nearly a decade now, taking care of him, keeping him safe, and allowing him more freedom than anyone else had ever given him. Even though he worked for Medane, at times it felt like a more paternal relationship and Raven knew that Medane was the father he never had. He couldn't ask the closest thing to a parent he had to kill himself, even if it would save the woman he loved. He couldn't choose either of them, so he didn't act and by his inaction he knew he was dooming Nalia to death.

His lack of action ate away at him as he lay in the darkness and shut his eyes against her steady breathing. Usually her breathing was soothing—a sign that the end had not yet come. But tonight it was an accusation and he knew that he would never fully recover from her death, because he was solely responsible. He had the cure, the solution, and he refused to act. He heard movement in the darkness but kept his eyes closed. Often Nalia's friend Jess came to see her, though not usually at night. Still, it wasn't uncommon for one of the rebels to stop by and they tried not to wake Raven. He didn't tell them that it didn't matter; he hadn't slept since landing despite his exhaustion and the bullet hole in his gut.

He still wasn't sure how he survived long enough to crawl back to the car and set off the distress signal, let alone how he had stayed conscious the grueling hours until help had arrived, but he had. They had bandaged him up and given him blood, and sent him to Medane and Nalia. He shivered as he remembered his first sight of Nalia. Like a sleeping beauty, only no kiss could wake her up.

There was a muffled grunt of pain from Nalia's bed—not her—and Raven sat up.

"Who's there?"

Silence. The room was empty. Raven got to his feet and checked for signs of an intruder. Nalia lay still and silent as always, with her slowly burning arm on top of the covers. Raven frowned. He had left both of her arms under the covers to protect her from the ash that still hung in the air when the wind rose up. He lifted her arm and gasped. The bracelet was gone.

Medane.

Raven ran to the door just in time to see the shadow of a díamont lumbering towards NeoLondon. He winced. He was in no condition for a chase, but he had to stop Medane. Medane had removed the bracelet but he wasn't dead yet, so if Medane could just drop the bracelet, then perhaps this nightmare would be over. Raven shuffled out the door after Medane, knowing he was losing speed on the díamont even though Medane paused frequently. The pain must be excruciating, Raven thought, and forced his feet faster. They reached the edge of Díamont Crater and Medane stopped.

"Medane!"

The díamont turned and even through the diamond sheathing his face, Raven saw surprise reflected in his features.

"Don't worry, Raven," Medane said in a pained voice. "The world is yours now."

Raven took another step and a flare of light surrounded Medane. The díamont's body was on fire and Medane looked to the empty sky and pointed up. Then a blue stream of light shot up into the sky. Raven gasped. Atheus had said there would be an explosion, but Nalia had been able to control it. Would Medane be able to control his death to prevent NeoLondon from suffering another strike?

Just as the blue light began to fade, an enormous white wall seemed to slam out from Medane and struck Raven, flinging him backwards against a half-destroyed pillar. He blinked, but his vision was gone. Where was Medane? What had happened? He couldn't see anything, and the force of the blow had reopened his wound. He collapsed to the ground and crawled forward, hoping to feel Medane. His fingers closed upon a bracelet in a pile of ashes. The bracelet was ice cold.

FOR TWO DAYS Lethe had followed Atheus, growing more and more desperate. There could be no doubt now: Atheus was behind the bombing on NeoLondon and more devastation was on its way. But the humans were the ones initiating the attacks, and it had always been Lethe's policy to stay out of human affairs. He longed to leap out of the shadows and kill Atheus before more cities were wiped out, but that would leave Medane the only díamont and such power might corrupt the otherwise cooperating díamont. He had to figure out how to lure Medane and Atheus to the same location so that both could be killed, but he knew Atheus would never agree. Atheus was openly flaunting the laws Lethe had set into place; he would never willingly give up his life.

Moscow was bombed, and in retaliation he heard that the Eastern World was preparing a strike on a major city. So far the East had only attacked half-abandoned cities like Los Angeles with minimal casualties, but nearly thirty million people had been killed in the strike on Moscow, which was completely unprepared for a nuclear strike. Even Lethe understood that the humans would want significant payback for such a tragedy.

Atheus returned to Seattle on the second day after killing Kaela as if drawn to the location, and Lethe shadowed him. Lethe considered his options. He needed to deal with Atheus now, before any more damage was done. There was no more time to wait and see what would happen; real lives were being lost and the planet was spiraling into unstoppable war just as it had fifty years ago. Lethe had been created to stop that war, and he would stop this war as well. But he was afraid, because once Atheus and Medane were dead, he was programmed to take his own life and he had grown fond of living.

Lethe took a deep breath and stepped forward. Atheus turned and saw him, and lifted his hand as if to ward him away. A wall of white light flashed past Atheus and Lethe, knocking both of them to the ground. The buildings around them trembled and one collapsed into the crater where they stood. Lethe gasped.

His entire life, he had been able to feel Medane and Atheus. It was built into him so that he could always locate and destroy them if necessary. But suddenly, half of his awareness was gone. Medane was gone. There was only Atheus. He had fallen to his knees and he remained there for a long minute, dreading what he knew had happened. Medane had taken the bracelet. Medane was dead. It was just him and Atheus now. He looked up at Atheus and saw his shock and horror reflected there.

"I feel again, Lethe," Atheus said in a voice of wonder mixed with sorrow. "My brother is gone, and I feel his loss. What good are feelings when they hurt so much?"

"You feel his loss because you loved him," Lethe said, realizing with surprise that he had loved Medane too. "Don't you remember the love? Or is it just the pain that you feel?"

"Love is weakness," Atheus said. "Soren was right. We were meant to be gods, but our love crippled us. And now, without Medane—what good is being a god if you're alone?"

Lethe saw his chance. "You won't have to worry about being a god or being alone, Atheus. Give me your hand as you offered decades ago, and let me take away your pain."

Atheus hesitated and looked around the bombed out city as if searching for escape. They both knew there was none. Lethe was designed to be lighter and faster than the other díamonts and the slightest touch was all that was needed to start the process. With Atheus firmly in his sights, there was no escape. But still, he wanted this to be a decision that Atheus made for himself, as Medane had done. He didn't want to murder his friends, the only two people he now realized he had ever loved.

"That's it, isn't it," Atheus whispered. "All the planning, all the games, and it's over. I could have been immortal."

"I never would have allowed it."

"You would have, if Medane had gone along with it, if he had become immortal as well. The three of us, living forever with the humans serving and amusing us."

"Is that all you think of the humans?"

"That's all they think of us. They wanted toys and when they saw how dangerous we were, they tried to destroy us. Us, the very gods they had created!"

"You sound like Soren," Lethe said, remembering the tapes of Soren's speeches he had heard. He shook his head. "I should have known from the way you refer to the Last War. When Medane says it, he means the final war, but when you say it, you mean the previous war. You always planned on this happening, didn't you? Another war, another chance to wipe out the humans and turn the díamonts into gods."

"What else could happen?" Atheus asked. "The humans will never be happy with peace. Look how eagerly they jump at the chance to bomb each other. They just need a leader. Medane wouldn't be a leader for his people, and now his people are dying."

"They will have a leader, and that leader will make sure that this war ends without any more bloodshed," Lethe said. "But that is for the humans to decide. We've interfered in their lives enough. Come here, Atheus. Don't make me come to you."

Atheus's eyes narrowed and for a moment, he looked like he was going to run. Lethe tensed, preparing to chase. Then Atheus sagged, and it looked like the fight went out of him.

"He's really gone, isn't he? Medane is never coming back. My brother. I planned for this day, thought I would be happy to rid the world of him, but now I find that I don't want to live without him."

Lethe stretched out his hand without a word. Atheus approached, and placed his palm in Lethe's. Instantly Atheus tried to retrieve his hand as the burning began, but Lethe clamped down on him. Atheus started screaming as his arm burned to ashes in Lethe's grip and Lethe took a few steps backwards. Atheus fell to the ground, writhing in agony, his screams gruesome in the night air as his entire body began to disintegrate, but not his consciousness, not until the very end. Then the world went silent and all that remained was a pile of ashes.

Lethe stared at what was once his friend, then stared at his hand. He had dreaded this moment his entire life, and had never really thought about what would happen next. But he was programmed and couldn't fight as his body moved of its own accord to take the pendant that always hung around his neck and place it on his tongue. It took several minutes for the sweet coating on the poison to wear away and Lethe took those last precious moments to remember Medane and Atheus in their youth, before the world corrupted them, when Atheus had will-ingly held out his hand, when the two of them had taught him basketball in the snow, when they had shared beers and secrets over an open flame, when the weight of the world didn't seem to matter as much because Soren was defeated and peace had returned.

Then the poison began to burn, and he shut his eyes and screamed.

CHAPTER 23

The lights in the plane flickered and Scott woke up. He was finally returning to the British islands after a whirlwind tour of the major Eastern cities, earning support for Bryce's presidency among the political elite. Most were eager to have him, since they had worked with him in the past, and the few who weren't eager at least respected him, since they had likely been at the other end of his gun before. He had booked this flight last minute and been disappointed to learn that it was an older model and the flight time to Windsor was nearly twice as long. Still, he estimated they were nearly there and he tried to relax his grip on the seat.

It seemed like he spent more time up in the air than on the ground ever since NeoLondon, and flying was a terrifying experience for him ever since Lydia's shuttle was caught in limbo. There was no news yet, although now at least he knew that the shuttle had made it out of orbit and would land on the moon soon. He thought of Lydia, trapped on a shuttle with barely any food and water for a week, waiting to crash into the moon and hope to survive long enough to be rescued. It was better than thinking of her already dead. He shuddered. So did the plane.

The plane dropped several feet and the passenger next to Scott came awake with a shriek. Scott grasped the arms of his seat with a death grip and looked around for some explanation. The flight attendants raced to the front of the plane and told everyone to buckle up. The plane trembled in the air, losing and gaining altitude abruptly. Scott kept his mouth firmly closed and stared fixedly at the front of the plane. Had Lydia felt this gut-wrenching helplessness?

Without warning, the lights went out. Outside the window, a white light stretched across the sky, momentarily blinding everyone. When Scott's vision cleared, the lights were still out. No backup lights came on in their place. Screams filled the darkness and Scott felt tears running down his cheeks. The flight attendants yelled at everyone to stay seated, buckle up, and stay calm, but chaos had already broken out. Luckily everyone was too scared to get up as the plane dropped further in the sky.

The earth seemed so close outside the window, far too close, and it was rising steadily to meet them. The trees were almost as tall as the plane. Then the plane crashed into the ground, sending everyone rushing to the ceiling. Skittering to the right, it bounced up into the air and crashed down again, slowing with each shuddering, screaming collision. Finally, there was silence, broken only by a drawn out wailing.

Scott opened his eyes and raised a hand to his head. There was blood on his fingers. His pelvis felt shattered, but he could move. One of the flight attendants managed to stand up and she urged people towards the emergency exits. She seemed to be trying very hard not to look at the other flight attendant, whose limp body lay in a pool of blood.

Scott managed to climb out of the plane and was surprised as he assessed the other survivors. Everyone was in bad shape, but most had survived. One woman carried a moaning blue bundle and his stomach twisted as a baby's hand reached out, but at least the baby was alive. His throat constricted as the flight attendant pulled a small girl screaming from plane. He didn't want to know where her parents were.

The land around them was heavily scarred by the plane, but it appeared to be farmland and mostly uninhabited. His hands shook as he took out his phone, and he frowned as he heard nothing. He checked, but the phone wasn't damaged in any way. It just wouldn't work. Could the cell network be down? He saw other people trying their phones with similar misfortune and a new thought struck him. The white light they had seen might have been an electromagnetic pulse, which destroyed anything that depended on electricity to run. EMP weapons had been developed, but none had ever been used. Had Atheus resorted to such means?

An EMP would mean more than just phones being down, it would mean that all of the cars, trains, and even airplanes would fail. The whole planet would be unable to communicate and chaos would reign. Scott wiped his brow and his hand came away slick with sweat and blood. Would all the work he had just put into uniting the Eastern World go to waste because Atheus managed to isolate everyone with a new weapon?

People started to show up from the nearby town and Scott was relieved when he saw doctor's coats along with the brightly clad farmers. As the two groups met, he recognized one of the women, a former writer for the paper. She paled when she saw him and took him to one side. She forced him to sit and washed and bandaged his head. She was biting her lip to hold back tears and he wondered how bad it was, but he didn't have time to be hurt. He needed to get to NeoLondon and Raven. Raven would know how to undo the EMP.

"What happened?" Scott asked.

"No one knows. A bright light, everything went dead, phones, computers, everything, and next thing we know a plane's falling out of the sky. You're so lucky to be alive."

"I need to get to NeoLondon."

"It's gone," she said, placing a cold cloth against his head as he winced in pain.

"Someone there can fix things," he said, not knowing how to explain any further. He was starting to get dizzy and he needed to reach NeoLondon quickly, before his injury caught up with him.

"I have an old fuel-cell car with enough fuel to get to NeoLondon. It might still work."

"Thank you," he said, and stood up. He ignored her protests and pushed past her as he headed into the small village nearby and found the car. She accompanied him, protesting the whole time, but she must have seen that this was important because in the end she gave him the key and a kiss, telling him to come back safely.

"I'll do my best," Scott said, holding her close for a moment and wondering if he would ever hold Lydia like this again. She would be proud of him, he thought. Pushing aside his own pain to help others. To help Raven. He shut his eyes and prayed that he found Raven alive.

RAVEN OPENED his eyes to the sound of someone calling his name. It was a familiar voice. For a moment, he forgot where he was and he remembered Scott calling him like this in an earlier time, after the massacre. He had often come to Díamont Crater to clear his mind, and he would stay for days sometimes until Scott came looking for him. But this time, there was no amusement in his friend's voice. There was panic. Sheer and utter panic, as if everything in his world was falling apart.

"I'm here," Raven called.

He didn't quite seem to be able to stand up and when he looked at himself he realized why. Blood seeped from where Atheus had shot him and his skin was dangerously pale. The rest of his body was covered in minor cuts as if he had been caught by shrapnel. He lifted a hand to his head but could only remember a white light, and nothing before it. His hand was covered in ash and he stared down at the bracelet on the ground before him. Then it hit. The memory of Medane, standing here, sending the gamma rays into the sky but unable to channel all of the energy safely away. Medane, who had cared for him like a father, gone forever.

A tear ran down his cheek just as Scott skidded to the top of nearby column and spotted him.

"Raven! You're alive!"

Scott leapt down beside him and stared at the bracelet curiously, but his attention was mostly on Raven. He immediately put pressure on the injury and started swearing.

"Of course you're injured. You don't know how to stay safe, do you?"

Scott scolded him lovingly and Raven wrapped his arms around the other man in a hug that Scott returned. Scott had a bandage on his head and Raven wondered what had happened. He tried to get to his feet and winced.

"What are you doing?" Scott asked. "I'll get people to come here."

"No," Raven said. "I can walk."

And he could, with support from Scott. He took one last look at Díamont Crater and the deceptively calm Lake Thames. Lifting the bracelet from the ground, he threw it into the lake with all the force he could muster. He would have thrown it in the sea if he could, but he didn't have the strength or the means.

He thought of Nalia, lying white as death in the rebel camp. Was she still alive, or had he waited too long and the damage become permanent? Tears ran down his cheeks as he thought of Medane's sacrifice being in vain and Nalia dying, but he clung to hope as tightly as he clung to Scott as they staggered out of the ruins together. Scott was trying to tell him something about power and electricity but all of his thoughts were on Nalia. Nothing else mattered.

They reached the camp and Raven stumbled to the tent where Nalia slept. She was still there, still pale and sleeping with burn marks twisting their way up her arm. He fell to his knees beside her and kissed her.

"Please, Nalia," he whispered. "Please wake up. I need you."

He laid his head on her chest while Scott called for doctors, but he wouldn't let the doctors come near. Not yet. Not until he was sure she wouldn't wake up. An hour passed and he began to grow faint. Black spots danced in his vision but Nalia hadn't changed. Scott pulled him away and there was sympathy in his eyes.

"Come on, Raven. The doctors need to look at you and a few minutes won't matter."

He nodded mutely and tried to stand, but he couldn't. Two doctors carried him into a nearby tent and took care of his injuries. They used low-tech devices to stitch him up and he idly wondered why they weren't using their usual assortment of instruments that healed almost instantly and left few scars, but he didn't ask. He didn't care. Nalia was still unconscious. He shut his eyes and fell asleep.

He didn't know how long he had been sleeping when he felt lips pressing against his. It must be a dream, he thought. A dream he didn't want to wake from. But there was something urgent being said to him, something he wanted to hear. His name, said in Nalia's voice, calling him back from the brink of some dangerous precipice.

"Raven," she whispered. "Don't go. I need you."

His words repeated back to him. He felt his eyes grow warm with tears and he opened them slowly. Nalia's face was before him and at the sight of her, he shut his eyes again. It was a dream, it had to be, and he couldn't wake up or he would lose her. He opened his eyes again and she was still there. She was smiling, and she kissed him again.

"Nalia," he said.

Then he became aware of other sounds, and other sights. Scott stood nearby, as did several doctors, all looking relieved. They were talking amongst themselves about his chances of survival and he realized with shock that he couldn't move. He must have been closer to death than he knew. He tried to look down at himself and see the damage, but his head was firmly wedged in place. He was no longer in a tent, he noticed, but a real room with concrete walls and ceiling. High-tech equipment stood attached to the walls, but it was turned off.

Nalia kissed him again while Scott gestured to the restraints holding him in place.

"He's awake, can you let him go now? We have so much to do."

"We can't rush the healing process—"

"I'm fine," Raven said between kisses.

His heart was leaping in his chest and he felt amazingly good. Medane's sacrifice had not been in vain. Because of Medane, Nalia was alive. But there was considerable fallout from his death that Raven knew he needed to deal with, and he wanted to get started as soon as possible. He knew that Scott and Medane had proposed him as the new president, and now was the time to take power, with Nalia at his side. He suddenly remembered what Scott had said about the electricity being out world-wide, and he was already thinking of ways to turn it to his advantage as he brought power back to the struggling planet. He would make Medane proud, and take good care of the world Medane had entrusted him with.

The doctors unbound him and he stood up slowly, not wanting to strain his body. For once, he actually cared about pushing himself too far. He was valuable, he realized. He had always thought of himself as disposable before, not worth taking care of, but now he knew that he needed to take care of himself for the planet's sake, for Medane's sake. He slowly walked out of the medical facility and saw the ruin of

NeoLondon in the distance. No other city would ever look like that, he vowed.

His fingers tangled around Nalia's and she smiled up at him. The wind picked up and howled around them, spiraling outward towards the deserted city as he leaned in for a kiss. The old world was gone, but their world was just beginning.

APPENDIX A: A BRIEF HISTORY OF THE LAST WAR (WWIII)

The third world war in recorded history, known as the Last War, began without warning at 7:28 am EST (UTC + 11) on October 27th, 2085 CE when an atomic bomb detonated approximately 600 feet above Sydney, Australia. Initial casualty estimates reached 500,000 on the first day, primarily caused by flash or flame burns and falling debris. Within one week the casualties rose past 1 million due to nuclear fallout and radiation sickness exacerbated by lack of medical attention.

A secret research faction of the United States of America (codename "Project Genome") revealed their successful attempt to create nonhuman superbeings and admitted that one of their three subjects had escaped, and that the escaped díamont, known as SOREN, was capable of cracking the codes protecting worldwide nuclear arsenals.

The Sydney atomic bomb was reported to have been fired by the United States of America. Subsequent research has found that the weapon was removed from United States control two days before the attack and given to a terrorist group under the direction of SOREN, díamont.

APPENDIX B: THE LAST WAR: A TIMELINE

2085 CE

- October 27th: an atomic bomb detonates over Sydney, Australia. Worldwide emergency is declared.
- October 28th: details of Project Genome are made public in an effort to prevent retaliatory attacks on the United States of America. The two díamonts still in United States custody, ATHEUS and MEDANE, are placed under emergency quarantine.
- October 29th: the United Nations meets to discuss the possibility of tracking down the rogue díamont.
- November 1st: a Russian nuclear weapon destroys Vancouver, Canada. Subsequent earthquakes lead to destabilization of Mount Rainier and vast lahars destroy much of the populous area surrounding Seattle, Washington, United States. Russia claims no knowledge of the attack. Emergency disarmament begins in all nations worldwide.
- November 2nd: a United States nuclear weapon is detonated over Brasilia, Brazil.

- November 3rd: the South American Freedom Army (SAFA) is formed and unites many of the nations in South and Central America against the United States. Sympathizers worldwide view the United States as the cause of the conflict although the United States maintains that it had no part in the nuclear attacks.
- November 4th: Texas secedes from the United States and joins SAFA.
- November 5th: Mexico joins SAFA. SAFA declares war on the United States.
- November 7th: the Catholic Pope addresses millions of viewers on television for the first time since the conflict started. Rogue díamont SOREN murders the Pope during the speech and declares that the Apocalypse has come. SOREN calls for widespread rebellion against governments supporting the United Nations, which he claims to be led by the Antichrist. Extremist Christian groups around the world take up arms and mass hysteria increases.
- November 13th: a second meeting of the United Nations is held. All governments worldwide are under siege. The United States begins work on a method of destroying díamonts, known as the LETHE PROJECT.
- November 25th: the last major government across the globe has been shut down. Power, heat, and clean water are limited in most areas and nonexistent in some due to worker strikes and sabotage.
- November 30th: the third meeting of the United Nations debates whether or not to give díamonts ATHEUS and MEDANE permission to leave quarantine in order to find and stop SOREN.
- December 1st: the United Nations formally releases ATHEUS and MEDANE from custody. The decision is hotly debated but the surviving government officials see no other option.
- December 13th: ATHEUS and MEDANE track down SOREN in London. MEDANE sets off one of the remaining nuclear devices and disables all díamonts.

2086 CE

- January 1st: SAFA spokespeople approach the United Nations and request an end to hostilities to prevent further nuclear war. Within hours, all remaining nations pledge their support in the Laos Treaty.
- January 28th: nations already united by SAFA as well as the United States and Canada form a United Western government, served by SAFA's army.
- January 30th: remaining nations in South and Central America join the United Western government in exchange for peacekeeping troops provided by SAFA.
- February 10th: nations in the African continent join in a Southern Alliance.
- February 13th: the area once known as Russia reunites under a common government and allows valuable heat to reach the northern areas and prevent further mass deaths due to weather extremes.
- March 5th: Europe reestablishes the European Union.
- March 9th: the United Western government sends SAFA troops to East Asia in an attempt to bring peace to the area.
- March 14th: the United Western government sends SAFA troops to the Middle East for similar peacekeeping missions.
- March 18th: China, Japan, South Korea, India, and a coalition of Middle Eastern nations declare war on the new United Western government in retaliation for unwanted peacekeeping efforts.
- March 20th: SAFA troops begin withdrawing from the Middle East and East Asia to prevent nuclear retaliation.
- April 5th: the United Western government ends all military involvement overseas.
- April 14th: a coalition of China, Japan, South Korea, India, and the Middle Eastern coalition invites remaining Asian nations, Europe, Russian, the Southern Alliance, Australia, and the South Pacific to join them in a grand United Eastern government.

- April 30th: the last of the remaining Asian nations joins the United Eastern government.
- June 1st: Russia joins the United Eastern government.
- June 14th: the Southern Alliance joins the United Eastern government after peacekeeping missions from the United Eastern government drastically reduce warfare and improve healthcare in Lower and Upper Africa.
- June 18th: all nations in the South Pacific unanimously agree to join the United Eastern government.
- June 29th: Australia refuses to join and United Eastern government troops invade.
- August 11th: Australia's existing government is toppled and Australia becomes part of the United Eastern government.
- September 30th: initial work on PROJECT LETHE is completed and ATHEUS and MEDANE are given permission to survive by the United Western government.

2087 CE

- May 31st: the European Union is the only government not part of a world government and is pressured to join the United Eastern World. Negotiations to join begin.
- October 27th: the Sydney Peace Accord is proposed, two years after the third world war began. The main proposals: worldwide peace will be assured by the establishment of two world governments, to be divided by oceans, namely the United Western World, composed of the American continents and nearby islands, and the United Eastern World, composed of Eurasia, Africa, Australia, and the South Pacific; Research on díamonts will be forbidden; Conflicts between nations within each world government must be dealt with by the world government and not escalate into another world war.
- November 3rd: negotiations between the European Union and the United Eastern World come to a standstill when the European Union refuses to join unless Europe is considered the primary nation-state of the world government.

2088 CE

- January 5th: NeoLondon is chosen as the capitol of the United Eastern World and the European Union officially joins the United Eastern World.
- January 6th: the Sydney Peace Accord is signed and put into law.
- January 16th: the LETHE PROJECT is complete.
- January 17th: LETHE, a díamont, kills SOREN and officially declares the Last War over.

APPENDIX C: PROJECT GENOME: DÍAMONT BRANCH

T his report has been compiled for personal use only. Information included in this report cannot be used in federal investigations to prove knowledge of wrongdoing. Information current as of 12.1.2134.

PROJECT GENOME: Díamont Research Branch was formally closed 10.29.2085. The Lethe Project was formally closed on 1.16.2088. Any research beyond those dates on the production or destruction of Díamonts is strictly forbidden. Violators will be put to death under Section 142F of the Sydney Peace Accord (1.6.2088).

RESULTS:

Soren. FAILURE. First díamont. Created 1.24.2067. Genetic enhancements introduced in the first trimester of carrier's pregnancy. Able to switch between human and díamont form successfully until the age of 14. Inability to leave díamont form resulted in severe emotional disconnect and delusions.

Historical Notes: Escaped the Genome Compound 10.15.2085. Successfully detonated three nuclear bombs. Appeared at the Vatican 11.7.2085 and committed televised murder. Responsible for mass genocide across the globe. Captured 12.13.2085 in London with assistance from Atheus (díamont) and Medane (díamont). Destroyed by Lethe (díamont, Lethe Project) 1.17.2088.

ATHEUS. SUCCESS. Second díamont. Created 2.19.2067. Genetic enhancements introduced in the third trimester of carrier's pregnancy. Able to switch between human and díamont form successfully. Currently involved in the government of the United Western World. Scheduled to be put to death by Lethe (díamont, Lethe Project) at first signs of mental instability.

MEDANE. SUCCESS. Third díamont. Created 4.2.2067. Genetic enhancements introduced in the third trimester of carrier's pregnancy. Able to switch between human and díamont form successfully. Currently involved in the government of the United Eastern World. Scheduled to be put to death by Lethe (díamont, Lethe Project) at first signs of mental instability.

ABOUT THE AUTHOR

Anne Elizabeth Winchell is an author, gamer, artist, and teacher. She grew up in Spokane, Washington and began writing speculative fiction in elementary school. Her passion for science fiction and fantasy led her to Texas State University, where she earned an MFA in Creative Writing and went on to teach creative writing and video game studies. In her spare time, Winchell designs and sells 3D digital models for use in art, film, and video games.

twitter.com/lilaeris_9

ALSO BY
ANNE ELIZABETH WINCHELL

DYSTOPIAN GALAXIES: VISIONS OF THE FUTURE

Dystopian Galaxies is a collection of twelve unrelated stories and poems that explore different visions of what the future might be like after humanity has expanded beyond Earth. Although none of the stories take place in the same galaxy, they share a theme of unchanging human nature and the dangers of refusing to adapt to a shifting world. While several offer hope of change and reconciliation, others warn against the drastic consequences of failing to learn from past mistakes.

Love, family, and hope are explored in a variety of worlds, ranging from inhospitable earths where people are crammed into cities of millions and the only hope comes from alien gold, to a legendary mountain range whose unnatural stability is challenged by the forces of technology that threaten an avalanche. From plagues that warp DNA to raids that threaten the lives of innocents, the dystopian futures imagined in this collection will inspire and provoke.

Dystopian Galaxies: Visions of the Future is available for eBook on Amazon Kindle and Kindle Unlimited, and in print on Amazon.

THE MOON OF LYCCA

When Mei is stranded during an evacuation of one of the most dangerous planets in the galaxy, she must rely on her speed and wits to survive both the alien world and the hostile creatures hunting her. But as she fights for her life, the planet has several unexpected surprises for her and she begins to realize that surviving on the moon of Lycca will be more challenging than just surviving the deadly creatures who only emerge at night.

The Moon of Lycca is available for eBook only on Amazon Kindle and Kindle Unlimited.